W9-DAP-742

THE DARKLING

For Nathalie, Cecily, and Nathaniel

THE DARKLING

Charles Butler

Margaret K. McElderry Books

Margaret K. McElderry Books
An imprint of Simon & Schuster Children's Publishing Division
1230 Avenue of the Americas
New York, NY 10020

Book design by Nina Barnett
The text of this book was set in Perpetua.

Printed in the United States of America

10 9 8 7 6 5 4 3 2 1

Library of Congress Cataloging-in-Publication Data:
Butler, Charles.
The darkling / Charles Butler.
p. cm.
Summary: As her father seems to be getting his life together two years
after her mother's death, fifteen-year-old Petra has a strange encounter with an eccentric
old recluse that somehow links her and her father to a tragic past love affair.
ISBN 0-689-81796-7
[1. Supernatural—Fiction. 2. Grief—Fiction. 3. Fathers and daughters—Fiction.] I. Title.
PZ7.B9745Dar   1998
[Fic]—dc21
97-30232
CIP   AC

Contents

Contents (continued)

THE DARKLING

1

Trick or Treat?

I'VE BEEN LYING HERE for hours now—wondering about the best way to tell you. It's a story that hasn't ended yet, so where do I begin? All those years back, with Edmund Century and his secrets? The night Eurydice died? Or just three Halloweens ago, when Harlow sprang his little surprise on me? You see my problem: I'm spoiled for choice. There are too many ways into this story. Too many ways in, and for some of us no way out at all. It isn't fair.

Well, let's start with Mr. Harlow and his stupid package. I'll be glad to see the back of him.

I was late that day, I remember. I usually was. From our house on The Rise to the Composers' Estate was a ten-minute ride, and from there to Harlow's shop was another four, even cutting across the Common. Still, I was surprised when I arrived at the newsagent's to find the street lamps already glowing and the old Benson & Hedges sign flickering above the window. I propped my bike against a pile of milk crates. Late as I was, I paused to skim the ad cards in the window. Dad was usually after some piece of junk—car spares, secondhand tools and stuff—

and occasionally I could spot a bargain. Right at the bottom was a card in my own writing:

Reliable girl, 15, available for baby-sitting.
Why wait till they leave home?
Have a night out while you can still enjoy it!
Call Cooper's Bridge, 750534
(ask for Petra)

I can do lovely handwriting when I try, and this card was very neat, in green felt-tip with curly bits around the capital letters. The last line looked like it was squeezed in as an afterthought (it was), but I thought it was the kind of ad that would do good business—or might have been if Mr. Harlow hadn't chosen to stick it six inches off the ground. No one but a midget would see it down there, and the midgets of Cooper's Bridge didn't seem to trust me with their children.

Through the window I could see Harlow, working at his ledger. He looked up, and for a moment our eyes met, but there was nothing romantic about it, thank goodness. I knew for a fact that he'd been married three times, so perhaps he had hidden attractions. But then he'd been divorced three times, too, so probably not. Harlow was bald, thin, and wore unfriendly spectacles. His specs were *unsympathetic*—tinted lenses, made for hiding behind. You can't trust a man who wears specs like that, especially when you see his eyelashes twitch like net curtains behind the glass.

"Hello, Mr. Harlow." The door rattled; the bell clattered. There was no way of getting into that shop quietly.

Harlow glanced up as if he'd only just noticed I was there.

"This is the second time this week," said the voice behind the specs.

"I know, I'm sorry. I couldn't find my bike lights."

"If you'd come when you ought to, you wouldn't need lights. It was broad daylight half an hour ago."

This was quite true. But I couldn't help it. I did have to go home to change out of my school uniform after all, and the house was a long way off—fourteen minutes by bike. Then my dad would always pop out of his workshop to say a few words, which in those days meant a lot of words by the end. And besides, living in our house just *meant* everything took more time. Mine was one of those rooms where nothing stayed put. Shirts lurked under pillows; jeans crept off to sulk behind the wardrobe.

"It won't happen again," I said, catching Harlow with the full force of my winning smile.

"Well, you're here now." He handed me an orange bag with the evening papers. I looked them over. The *Cooper's Bridge Argus* for the most part, seasoned with circulars from the local supermarket. Not bad for a Friday.

Mine was an easy paper route—which meant it was a sensible shape, with straight streets laced neatly together and short garden paths to walk up instead of long driveways. The only dogs were friendly mutts I knew by name, who slobbered over me if I let them. On a good day I could zigzag my way back to the shop in forty minutes.

But this didn't turn out to be a good day.

"I almost forgot," said Mr. Harlow as I was turning to go. He produced a green paper package from behind the counter and smiled his dour smile back at me. "*The Spiritual Messenger.* For Mr. Century, up at the Hall."

"*Century Hall?* Does it really have to go tonight? I could take it there first thing Monday."

"Tonight. Mrs. Campbell has already been on the phone, and she was very insistent. Quickly now, the sooner you start the sooner you'll finish."

The lashes twitched triumphantly behind the tinted glass.

Sometimes I forgot that Century Hall was on my route at all. Old Mr. Century didn't take a daily or weekly paper. No magazines with old trains or knitting patterns found their way to the gray-stoned Hall. But about once a month, a package would arrive at Mr. Harlow's shop, and then my simple newspaper route would instantly stretch two miles—a mile up the hill to Century Hall and another mile back. Quite long enough to get soaked if it was raining (and it looked like rain now).

I delivered the other papers more quickly than usual. Elgar Drive, Sibelius Avenue, Britten Way, Bach Gardens. By twenty to six I'd made it to Manor Lane. I wanted to get to Century Hall before it was completely dark.

I can just remember a time before the Composers' Estate existed, when there was woodland on either side of Manor Lane, with secret shadowy paths and clearings. But for most of my life it had been like this: red tiles and porthole windows, and a hatchback in every drive. They were all around Cooper's Bridge, the new houses. For the moment, though, the Composers' Estate was the outer limit. Halfway down Manor Lane, the developers had paused for breath, and there the countryside erupted, right next to a row of back gardens.

Manor Lane gave up being a proper road and became a shabby rutted track, with moss running up the middle instead of white lines. A little farther and it began to climb, and then to twist up and around like a snail's shell, until it spiraled away from the town entirely and reached the summit of a wooded hill. And in that sudden wildness stood Century Hall, home of ghosts and shadows.

The lane was too steep to ride, so I chained my bike to a post, removed the light, and walked, the orange bag slung across my shoulder. As I left the lighted part of the street, a group of kids came out, dressed for Halloween in witchy hats and bony masks. I'd forgotten the date until then and was sorry to have been reminded—I was nervous enough already. I examined Mr. Century's package—still just enough light for that. It was encased in thick green paper, with an embossed pattern of leaves and flowers. Perhaps expensive birthday wrapping, or wallpaper plundered from an old-fashioned front parlor. Mr. Harlow had scribbled "Century Hall" on it in ballpoint, but that was all. In fact, when I came to look at it, there was already a small tear in the paper, which if I inserted my fingers . . .

"Blast!"

The tear was twice as big now, and I hastily put the package back. Not, however, without noticing the picture that had been partly revealed. It showed an hourglass, an old-fashioned one with UBI SUNT carved at the top and bottom. The sands had almost run through, and someone was reaching to turn it over—an ancient someone, with fingers like knotted twigs. Something about that hand made me glad I had not seen the rest.

By the time I reached the top of the hill, I was using my bike light to guide me. Down the long beech avenue to the gates, then through into the courtyard of Century Hall. The Hall was shaped like three sides of a square: a central part, with a grand stone porch in the middle, and two long arms that stretched out to greet visitors in a stiff embrace. One wing had housed the stables, but its doors were bolted and barred, the horses sold off years ago. Just a few wisps of straw were blowing about the cobbles. Pity—I was fond of horses. The other was no more than a ruin, gutted by a fire that had ripped through it, who could say how many years before? Now it was home to owls and rats and other things besides, all (I guessed) watching through the blackened window frames as I passed. Beside the porch a small keyhole of light shone out between drawn curtains.

Somewhere behind those curtains sat Mr. Century. In all my visits I had never seen him, though I'd heard the stories. A tragic love affair. A disfiguring accident. A bereavement. Everyone seemed to have their own account of him, but they all ended the same way: with Mr. Century alone in his fortress of a house, watching the years furl and unfurl outside his window, growing old as his name.

I stepped onto the porch. There was no mailbox and my first thought was to leave the package outside and make a quick getaway. I was actually leaning down to wedge it against the rusting boot scraper when I remembered it was meant to be urgent. I ought at least let Mr. Century know I had come. But there was no doorbell, only a long metal rod that hung down from the top of the porch to end at the level of my head. I pulled on it, and at once a bell chimed somewhere high above me. The sound carried into the shadowed woods. I would have called it back if I'd been able to.

I waited, hoping no one would answer. But the door opened, and Mr. Century's housekeeper was facing me.

"Yes, what is it?"

I knew her from the streets of Cooper's Bridge: a small, worried-looking Scotswoman, whose gray eyes constantly darted about as if she were afraid of being snatched up by a passing eagle. A gray cardigan hung limply over her shoulders like a shawl. In fact she seemed to consist entirely of gray: gray skirt, gray shoes and stockings—even her skin had a discolored tinge that made it look like papier-mâché. Newspaper and flour paste, all the way down.

"What is it?" she repeated.

"I've brought this for Mr. Century. There isn't any mailbox, you see, and it looked like rain, so I thought—"

"*The Spiritual Messenger?* Thank you, I'll tell him." She took the package and began to shut the door, but was interrupted by the tinkling of another small bell, this time from inside the house. "That's Mr. Century," she explained. "I'll see what he needs. You'd better wait here."

She disappeared, and I waited as I had been told, although I hardly knew why. It was getting darker every minute, and I wanted to be at home in the electric warmth of our living room, with the TV on and one of Dad's special stews on a tray. At last the housekeeper returned. "Mr. Century wishes to speak with you," she said. "Would you like to come this way?"

Not really, but I couldn't quite think how to refuse, and I found myself following her into a dark hallway. The only light came from an elegant oil lamp, although this was reflected to ghostly infinity in the glass of two heavy mirrors. The housekeeper seemed quite at home here, but I was already regretting the whole adventure. Too many of the black-and-white films I'd watched on Saturday nights featured young heroines being lured into houses just like this one by servants whose restless eyes concealed an age-old secret.

She opened a nearby door and waited expectantly as I entered.

The first thing I noticed was the heat. It rolled out in fierce waves from a log fire—stifling, unbearable in the airless room. Vases full of dried flowers, paperweights entombing skeletons of coral, a carriage clock with clawed brass feet, gilt-framed paintings of stags and Highland cattle, all were jostling for space. On a round table an ivory chess set lay abandoned halfway through a game, tiny gemstones glinting in the knights' eyes. Then I spotted Mr. Century. He was reclining in a chair beside the fire, his feet perched on a low ottoman, his body swaddled in blankets. If I hadn't known who this person was, I would have found it hard to tell whether he was man or woman. His face was turned to the fireplace, and further hidden by the flaps of a nightcap. All that protruded from the blankets was a long, delicate hand.

"Come here where I can see you, girl," said Mr. Century. "Campbell, shut the door; she's brought in a most foul draft."

At this point I decided—too late—that I did not want to be here. I turned to leave, just in time to see the door close firmly.

"I thought I told you to come here," said Mr. Century.

I stepped a little closer. Partly by the light of the fire and partly by a nearby oil lamp (there seemed to be no electricity in the Hall), I made out the face that was now regarding me with a cold, appraising stare. It was very, very old. The eyes were pale and watery, the lips drawn thin, the long nose sharp as a blade.

"No, no," he murmured. "I had thought there was something in the voice, but at such a distance . . ." It seemed I had been a terrible disappointment to him. Then he added more distinctly, as if he didn't believe I had heard his first remarks, "You see I am an invalid and do not mix much in the world. Forgive me if my manners seem antique. And what is your name, my dear?"

"Petra McCoy. Look, is there anything the matter? If it's to do with the—"

"Petra," repeated Mr. Century, then startled me by reciting, as loudly as he could:

> *Match me such marvel save in Eastern clime,*
> *A rose-red city—half as old as time!*

"Are your parents fond of the poets?" he asked in his normal voice.

"Not that I've noticed," I said. I'd managed to sneak a look at my watch as Mr. Century was speaking. It was already nearly six.

"So much the worse for them," he said curtly, but he looked at me with more interest than before. He took a poker from the hearth and prodded at the red heart of the fire. The sleeve of his dressing gown slid back, and I watched the muscles draw up his loose skin as though it were being hung on a line to dry. The logs shifted and sighed.

"You find this old body of mine fascinating, do you not?" he said, without looking around. "How can such an unlikely assemblage possibly hang together? Can it survive as much as another day? Oh, I remember how youth looks on at age in horror. I have the advantage of you there, as you have of me in so many things.

Just how old do you suppose I am, girl?"

"I really don't know," I began.

"On my next birthday, I shall be one hundred and two," he declared. "You see, I have already outlived my name!" At this he made a noise that began, perhaps, as a kind of triumphant chuckle but quickly fell into a racking cough. He tilted his head toward me, suddenly drained. "You cannot begin to guess how long a time that is."

I wasn't about to try.

"When your father was a boy, I was already an old man, by most people's reckoning. But the vigor I had then! If I could recapture a quarter of it . . . And now I begin to think I shan't see another spring."

"I'm sure you will," I said, although I thought he was probably right.

"Well, you are kind. Over the years I have thought of these matters. There may be ways, indeed. But after so long, it will be hard . . ." As he muttered to himself, his hands clasped and unclasped each other fidgetingly, and his eyes, which had been focused so sharply on me, strayed to the corner of the room.

I backed away, wondering if I should alert Mrs. Campbell as I left. Then a sound behind me took me by surprise: the voice of a grandfather clock announcing first the Westminster chimes, then six mellow hours.

"Don't leave me!" said Mr. Century in alarm. "I haven't given you your present."

"My present?"

"Your tip, then—gratuity, what you will. I have so few people with whom to share my possessions, and I no longer seem capable of enjoying them myself."

I returned to his side, curious in spite of everything. Mr. Century took my hand and pressed a flat object into my palm. "For my Hermes," he said emphatically. Then, seeing my blank expression, "The messenger of the gods—and you're a messenger of a kind, aren't you? Well, never mind. This belonged to the dearest friend of mine . . . which makes it precious, you know. If you take my advice, you'll keep it safe and read it seldom. Save it for a rainy day."

The thing in my hand was a book. It was no larger than a deck of cards, bound in calfskin, with peacock feathers etched at the borders. Across the center was printed in heavy gold letters, *The Rubaiyat of Omar Khayyam.* I opened it and flicked politely through the pages of ornate verse. Inside the cover ran an inscription: *To Eurydice, undying love—E.C.*

"Thank you," I mumbled, and wondered what else there could be to say; but Mr. Century solved that problem by announcing that he felt tired and needed rest. At once Mrs. Campbell appeared, so promptly that I guessed she had been standing by the door the whole time. Before I had a chance to say good-bye, she had hustled me from the room, through the dark hallway, and outside, the book still in my hand. I watched the rain drip from the ivy on the porch.

"I'm saving it for a rainy day," I commented to the boot scraper. Then I pulled up the hood of my raincoat and set off down the hill to find my bike.

2

No One Flies to Rio

MY DAD USED TO BE a man of bright ideas, and one of them was to fix a row of hooks to a beam above the kitchen sink, where coats and umbrellas might drip undisturbed. When I got home I took off my raincoat to hang it there, but the sink was full of debris from dinner.

"Jamie!"

There was no reply from the living room—just the tinny sound of applause on the television. For some reason this was more annoying than mere silence.

"Jamie!" I shouted. "Why haven't you done the washing up?"

"It's not my turn," he replied.

"It *is* your turn. Fridays, Saturdays, and Wednesdays—it's in the Contract."

"Give it a rest, won't you? I had a lot of homework."

"Just come out here and do it."

"All right. Later."

"Now, Jamie, I want to hang up my coat."

"I said I'd do it later. You can't order me about—can she, Dad?"

Dad sighed. He never enjoyed being referee. "Look, *I'll* do it this time, okay? And stop bickering, you two. If you must have an argument, at least conduct it in the same room."

I did the washing up myself. I knew Dad should have ruled in my favor, and I wanted to show them both how I could rise above petty selfishness. I did not change out of my wet jeans, but let my legs steam sacrificially as I sat in front of the electric fire with my dinner.

"You really ought to change," said Dad. "You don't want to get a cold. Jamie's already coming down with something."

"I know all about that. Wanted to get out of biology homework, did you, Jamie?"

"I did not!" cried Jamie, who was appalled at the idea of being ill over half-term holiday. "At least I don't smell like a wet dog," he added halfheartedly.

"It was when I was coming back from Century Hall it really started bucketing. That lane practically turns into a stream in bad weather."

"You went to Century Hall?" asked Dad. "Tonight?"

"That's why I'm late—it was one of those stupid parcels again."

"You shouldn't have gone up that lane after dark," he chided me. "It's not lit, is it? I'm amazed Harlow let you do it."

"Made me do it, more like," I said with my mouth full. "I wanted to leave it till Monday."

"Did you? Well, I shall be having a word with him about that."

"No you won't, Dad!" I protested, realizing that I had made a tactical mistake. "I'm in enough trouble with him already. It wasn't his fault I was late."

"I don't care about that. It's no excuse to send my daughter along a dark lane at night, and I shall tell him so."

"No, Dad! I'll lose my job if you go in all guns blazing." I reached up and made him look at me. "You know we can't afford to do without that money."

"And I can't afford to have anything happen to you," said Dad at length, but in a harrumphing voice that meant he would not press the point.

Jamie retched.

"And who asked you?" Dad ruffled Jamie's hair where he was leaning his head against the arm of the chair. His short burst of anger against Harlow was already blowing itself out, as I had known it would.

"Look what Mr. Century gave me," I said, hoping to lure his thoughts into a new channel. "He invited me in—said it was a tip."

"So you actually got to meet him! And I thought he spent all day dreaming about his lovelorn past." He examined the book. "Poetry—and nicely bound as well! Might be worth a shilling or two." He read some of the verses, nodding as if he knew them all by heart. "Can't say I see the appeal myself," he commented as he returned it. "But it was a nice gesture."

"This woman's going to win the holiday of a lifetime in a minute," cried Jamie, "and all you can talk about is some measly old *book!*" He turned up the volume on the remote control.

"But why did Mr. Century give it to me?" I asked.

"Who knows? Let's face it, he's probably not firing on all cylinders by now. Shut up all those years, with just that house-keeper for company."

"Not very good company, either," I muttered.

"You know, I don't suppose he's seen more than half a dozen people in the last thirty years. Just that Mrs. Campbell, the doctor, the postman—and now you. So you see, you're honored."

"I'm wet. Wet and tired, and fed up with this stupid program. Jamie, turn it down, will you?"

"Shh, listen! She's got to answer this one to stand any chance of going to Brazil."

The contestant never made it to Brazil, but for a while she did take my mind off Century Hall. It was only when I was getting ready for bed that I remembered Mr. Century. As I flung my jeans onto my chair, the book tumbled out of the pocket. With a heavy heart I realized that it was destined to join the ranks of the Indisposables—that growing band of dubious possessions I neither truly wanted nor could bring myself to throw away. I had dozens of them: furry animals won at fairgrounds, novelty key rings, pens that had run dry but might in time be persuaded to write again, a packet of Extra Strong Mints (*I* did not care for them, but maybe somebody would, one day), odd socks for use in emergencies only. They littered my room, in no kind of order, for none belonged with any of the others. I surveyed the mess with a kind of calm despair: for a moment it reminded me of Mr. Century's cluttered drawing room. "And where do *I* fit in?" I said out loud, as I retrieved the book and blew the dust off it.

> *Awake! for Morning in the Bowl of Night*
> *Has flung the Stone that puts the Stars to Flight:*
> *And Lo! the Hunter of the East has caught*
> *The Sultan's Turret in a Noose of Light.*

Hmm. I put the book in the black casket I kept on the dressing table. It was a little treasure chest inlaid with oriental flowers in mother-of-pearl, but contained nothing more valuable than a few safety pins and a brooch that had once belonged to my mum. I closed the lid carefully and pressed down the catch.

Mum would never have allowed the room to slide into such a state, I reflected. Dad tried his best, but he was just as disorganized as I was, and as for Jamie . . .

"Not a tidy bone between the three of you," said Mum inside my head. "I don't know what you'd do if you didn't have me to clean up after you."

And now we didn't have her, and so we did know. The house was going to rack and ruin, that was all. Chaos was seeping in through every unplugged crack. Dad's workshop had spilled into the kitchen, dominated for the last three weeks by a grease-encrusted car engine. Outside, the grass was uncut, and creepers were beginning to tap at the windows like man-eating plants in a sci-fi movie.

I sat and stared into the mirror. At the Borough Cemetery, the lawns were kept clear of weeds. The grass was short and neatly edged, and paths of chippings led from one immaculate plot to another. Each time we visited, it was like a standing reproach to our own garden and the jungle it had become in two short years. Resignedly I ran a hand through the tangle of my hair, still damp after the journey from Century Hall. I reached for the dryer and pointed it upward till the lank brown locks changed color and billowed wildly. I beat them back down with the brush, attacking with impatient strokes. But the long wisps flew up to meet the plastic and would not be settled, and in the

end I had to be content with something half subdued. My reflection stared back from the midst of this frizzy mane, a face
both small and solemn. And after all this, I was pleased with
the effect. Not Rapunzel perhaps, but something more mysterious—a halo seen through frosted glass.

When I was small, I had been afraid of the dark and had
evolved a bedtime ritual to keep its terrors at bay. Not three,
nor five, but exactly four steps were allowed to carry me from
the chair where I left my clothes to the bed; and then I must be
sure not to let a loose leg dangle over the edge while I was
putting on my pajamas, in case a clawed hand should reach out
and pull me to destruction. For years I had followed this proce-
dure earnestly, and then I had grown out of it, and for years
since had not given it a thought. But tonight the past was strong,
and I found myself going through the same actions, driven by the
same half-forgotten fears.

Once in bed I turned out the light and lay with my arms
folded across my breast. I was tired, but sleep was far away. The
rain splashed against the window, and the gutter, clogged with old
birds' nests, overflowed noisily onto the concrete below. A car's
tires hissed on the wet road. The street lamp threw shadows
against the curtain, and where the curtain sagged down from the
rod, the treetops moved in a small oval of light One branch quivered horizontally across the bottom of this patch. Another forked
in two directions from the top: two slanting eyes, set above a
thin-lipped mouth. It was just like a face—especially when
looked at squint-eyed. I smiled. I'd known it for years, this
shadow face that stared down from the ceiling. Tonight was no different: only the wind made its quivering mouth more talkative.

"Darkling," I said under my breath. It had come back to me, the last part of my nighttime ritual. The Darkling was the name I had given this face long ago. I murmured a charm to protect myself from whatever spells it might be chanting in its busy, silent language.

The Darkling's mouth quivered. "Ridashee." Half lost in the splash of water gulping from the overflow. "Ridashee . . . shidashee . . . shee . . ." I murmured my charm, and the wind dropped, and the Darkling's mouth grew obediently still. But outside the rain fell harder.

The water drained away under the streets, and the drains flowed like rivers in spate, unseen. On the hill outside Cooper's Bridge, a fresh gust blew rain through the windows of the burned-out wing. And a wavering candle lit Mrs. Campbell through the Hall as she made her rounds, checking each bolt and lock.

3

Good News from
the White Dragon

NEXT DAY I SAW MRS. CAMPBELL in the High
Street. It was a foggy Saturday morning, and at first I was aware
only of a small figure scuttling through the mist, hurrying from
door to door. Each time she reached the safety of a shop, she
paused and looked about nervously before moving on, as if
afraid the cars might swerve onto the pavement after her. As I
passed, she pushed against my arm, knocking me into the wall.

"Sorry," I said automatically, although the collision hadn't
been my fault. She started back, and it was only then that I recognized Mrs. Campbell—but before I could add more than a
strangled "Hello," she had slipped past, and I wasn't even sure
she had known me.

"Who was *that*?" asked my friend Mel, gazing after her.

"Nobody," I replied quickly. "Just one of the people on my
paper route. She lives up at Century Hall."

"Century Hall?" echoed Mel with a touch of scorn. "I should
have guessed. She'll be Igor's twin sister."

"What?"

"You must admit, that place has got a touch of Dracula's

Castle about it. All it needs is a few bats flitting about the rafters."
She shivered melodramatically. "Take some garlic next time."

"It's not *that* bad," I said, though why I should feel defensive
about Century Hall I could not imagine.

"Oh look, there's Daddy." Mel's father was waiting for us
outside Woolworth's. The door of the car was half open, and he
was waving at us to hurry. The engine was already running.

"Quick, I'm in a no-parking zone," he said. "You know this
street is crawling with police on a Saturday. What kept you?"

"We're here now," said Mel, climbing into the back. "Petra
was trying on hats in the market."

"Would you like a lift, Petra?" he asked, noticing me for the
first time.

"Of course she would. Get in, Petra."

"Thanks, Dr. Gaspard."

I followed Mel into the upholstered quiet of the car and
closed the door. At once the misty street was shut out, the
other shoppers reduced to wraiths. Inside the car was a different world, smelling of fur and plastic and Mel's father's aftershave. Warm air oozed around my fingers from a vent beside
the door.

I stroked the button that worked the automatic window. Our
car had never been as grand as this, but at least it had used to run.
There were times when I wished my dad could complete his end-
less tinkering with its insides, a process that had turned the kitchen
into a greasy operating theater and littered the draining board with
misshapen lumps of metal. If it wasn't that it gave him something
to do instead of brooding . . . Or perhaps it had become no more
than a way to give his brooding a different shape.

"And how is your father, Petra?" asked Dr. Gaspard as he pulled into the traffic. It seemed that some doctor's instinct had allowed him to read my thoughts, until he added: "Is he over that bout of flu yet?"

"He's fine. James is getting it now."

"Then you'll be next, if you don't watch out. Look after yourself. Prevention is better than cure."

"It's easy to see you're a doctor, Daddy, when you come out with gems like that," Mel said. "I hope you're listening, Petra."

"Yes," I said vaguely. But I wasn't. I was looking at Mrs. Campbell, who had just come into view again, entering a door at the corner of the High Street. I wiped the mist from the window and was able to make out the shape of a brass plate as we swept past. Dentist? Solicitor? Undertaker? The associations I had with brass plates were not pleasant.

"Can Petra come back for lunch?" Mel asked. "We could ride Hagar and Josh afterward."

"I don't see why not," replied Dr. Gaspard. "If she doesn't mind roughing it with the rest of us. You wouldn't turn your nose up at a bowl of soup and a roll, would you, Petra?"

"Of course not—but I can't. It's my turn to cook at home."

"That stupid Contract of yours!" said Mel. "You know you're the only one who takes any notice of it."

"I know. But that isn't the point."

"Besides, I thought you said Jamie had gone to stay with your gran."

"He has. Dad'll be waiting, though, and I promised to do him a fry-up."

"Well, you'll come to visit soon, won't you?" said Dr.

Gaspard. He gave me a quick smile in the rearview mirror. The smile matched his voice: benign, but dutiful. I knew that Dr. Gaspard could never understand how it was that his own daughter—clever, beautiful Melanie—had chosen to make so much of a friendship with someone as unremarkable as me. The truth was, I didn't understand it either. Mel was the natural center of any crowd, a flame to whom friends were drawn like so many moths. For a few weeks they would be inseparable, then she would tire of them, and they would fall away with their wings singed, vainly flapping for her attention. But between us the friendship had lasted, right from the time the Gaspards had moved to Cooper's Bridge eighteen months ago.

Dr. Gaspard dropped me off at The Rise. I stood and watched as his car swung around the circle at the end of the road, its headlights cutting a wide arc through the mist. Then it moved slowly down the sodden road and disappeared into traffic. I kicked my way through the weeds up to the front door.

As soon as I stepped inside, I could tell from the echo of my own feet that I was alone in the house. I hung up my coat and walked into the kitchen. It was silent, and cold with the faint, ineradicable chill that empty houses have. The breakfast things lay unwashed in the sink. An aroma of burnt toast lingered from a breakfast accident of Jamie's.

"Anyone home?"

I put the kettle on and went for the milk. The fridge door was covered with small magnets in novelty shapes: ballerina, slice of pizza, grinning clown's head. Each magnet held in place a sheaf of bills and offers. Behind the clown was concealed a grubby piece of paper, grandly entitled:

The McCoy Family Contract
THIS AGREEMENT IS BINDING IN LAW!

Article 5 of the Contract stated it very clearly: my own responsibility to make lunch on Saturdays, and the duty of other family members to give good warning if they weren't going to be there. I took out the milk and slammed the fridge door shut. The ballerina pirouetted to the floor, followed by a shower of final demands. For this I had given up a chance to go riding!

The Family Contract was my own idea, the latest attempt to stop life in the McCoy household from sliding irretrievably into chaos. Cleaning, cooking, laundry, washing up—each chore was carefully assigned, and after long negotiation I had persuaded Jamie and Dad to put their signatures to it. But I soon discovered that having something written down was no guarantee it would get done. Little by little jobs began to be postponed, resented, and eventually wriggled out of.

Stubbornly, I made lunch just as I had planned. Sausages and bacon were artistically arranged around a grilled tomato; a slice of fried bread looked on wanly. Dad's share went into the oven, and reluctantly I sat down to my own. I had studied nutrition at school and knew the harm that lurked in each ingredient. Lard! Death to the arteries. Fried bacon! Assault and battery on the complexion. I smiled. This was the way to end up like Mel's brother, Lee—the Zit King. Since no one ever saw Lee except the aliens who stared back at him from his computer, perhaps he didn't mind about his appearance. I did, however, and made a note to avoid fried foods for a week in compensation. But an agreement was an agreement. I took another bite of sausage and crackled the burnt bits against my tongue. Dad didn't know what he was missing.

Outside, the mist had finally cleared. A perfect day for riding, after all—and there was still time to get to Mel's if I took the bike. I washed and dried my hands, and sat cross-legged in front of the electric fire. Its single bar beat back ineffectually, and only my palms were warmed. No, I couldn't leave the house yet. Not until Dad came back. I needed to be sure he was okay.

Okay! At my age he should be the one waiting in for me. But so much of the recent past had been spent worrying about Dad, the habit was hard to break. I dived under the settee to retrieve the old magazines that had somehow got lodged there. Among them were the photo-romances I used to read ages ago, but today I discarded these in favor of Jamie's *Beano*.

I was distracted by the sound of the front door. Dad was grumbling as he went through his ritual struggle to wrest the key free of the lock.

"Hello, Petra!" he said affably. "You sitting here all on your owneo?" He looked very pleased with himself. This was certainly not the penitence I had been expecting. He bent down to peck the top of my head, and the smell of whiskey wafted with him.

I did not feel like returning the greeting. "Where have you been, Dad? Or need I ask?"

He looked at me for a moment, then laughed. "Very good! You only need a rolling pin and curlers and you could go on the stage."

"I've been waiting for you," I muttered.

"Is that so? I didn't realize I had a probation officer. I had a couple of drinks, all right?"

"Then you must be hungry."

"No, I had lunch in the pub," he explained with exaggerated patience. He started unbuttoning his raincoat, then froze, and clapped his hand to his forehead. "Oh dear. You were going to cook today, weren't you?"

I was suddenly fascinated by Dennis the Menace. "It's in the oven if you want it."

"I'm sorry, I really am. I plain forgot—I've had so much else on my mind."

"I can see *that*."

"Okay, I've said I'm sorry. Besides, I wasn't *only* having a drink, you know." He took his coat off and hung it under the stairs. "It was a business meeting," he added. He obviously had more to tell me, but now I would have to ask nicely.

"What business?"

"Oh, money business. Job business, to be precise." He looked at me out of the corner of his eye, and his affected nonchalance popped like a balloon. He slapped his hands on his knees and grinned. "I've got a job, Petra! A bona fide nine-to-five regular job!"

"A job? That's wonderful!" As I leaped to my feet, I found myself being lifted from the floor and swung around the room.

"Careful, Dad!" I cried as my heels trailed the edge of the fireplace.

"Okay, I give in," he said, putting me down clumsily. "Oh, my back! You're getting too big for that."

"Tell me all about it! What sort of job?"

"That's the best thing. It's draftsmanship, exactly what I'm trained for."

"Great! I mean, that's really great! But why didn't you tell me this chance was coming up?"

Now Dad was unstoppable. "I only heard about it myself this morning. That's why I had to rush off like that, to talk it over. You see, Graham Cooke is leaving Barlow's to set up his own practice, and he wants me to go in with him. I was the first person he thought of, he says. We've just been going over it all at the White Dragon. You're looking at the chief draftsman of Graham Cooke and Co., Architects to the Gentry. Of course, I'm also the only draftsman, but there's no need to stress that on the letterheads. What do you think, Petra?"

"Graham Cooke!" I repeated. I had stopped listening after that name.

"Petra, I know what you're going to say—"

"But he's the one who got you sacked from Barlow's in the first place!"

"Yes. Yes, of course. I know that."

"The man's a creep! The Creature in the Black Laguna, you used to call him. You can't go in with him!"

"Did I really?" Dad laughed. "The Creature in the Black Laguna. That's rather good, isn't it?"

"No, it's not rather good! It's terrible!"

I caught his attention at last. He breathed deeply and sat me down on the sofa beside him. "Look, Petra, I know you don't like him, and I know what I've said in the past. But I honestly think I was a bit hasty. I wasn't behaving very rationally after your mum died, you know. Just when Barlow's needed someone steady, there was I turning up late, being surly with clients—I wasn't exactly an advertisement for the firm. When they had to get rid of someone, I suppose I was the obvious choice."

"But that's just when they should have stood by you! After all the years you put in there."

"Maybe. Maybe. I know that's what I felt at the time. To tell you the truth, I think Graham feels a bit guilty about it. I think this job is partly his way of making amends. Not that I won't do good work, mind! I'm not quite a charity case yet."

"But Dad—"

"Petra!" he cut me off. "I've been out of work for over a year now. I'm not getting any younger. I *need* this job. And frankly, Graham's is the only offer I've had. Maybe we both deserve another chance, eh?"

"I suppose," I conceded.

Even so, I couldn't imagine Graham Cooke feeling guilty about anything. He was a smiling man with a voice as smooth as cream, but eyes that shifted restlessly, looking over your shoulder for advantage or escape. I had always disliked him: disliked the way he made Dad drink more than he could handle, the way his laugh would sharpen and cut the air like a saw when they were downstairs at the whiskey and I was lying in bed alone. And I disliked him for something else. Something Dad had never known about, and never must. Even now my mind slammed shut the door that led to that memory and took my thoughts a different way.

"He'll be paying you properly at least!" I said. "You know you're worth more than they gave you at Barlow's."

Dad looked a little bashful. "He can't do that, not at first. He's starting up a new business, remember. There are a lot of expenses. He hasn't even got his office set up properly—I'll be working from home some days. But I'm in on the ground floor! If we make a go of it, who knows where it might lead?"

"A Rolls for him, and maybe you'll get a pair of gold-plated bike clips when you retire. He's a sharp one, Dad! Just be careful."

He leaned back into the sofa and sighed. "I thought you'd be a bit pleased for me."

"But I am!" I protested.

"You don't sound it."

He was suddenly childlike, needing to be coaxed. I stared at his lined face gazing stubbornly into the woodwork—just like Jamie when he refused to be sent to bed. But Dad was too old for the sulks, and strangely enough that was the reason he must be indulged. I forgot what I had been going to say and took his hand. "Of course I'm pleased, Dad. It's just that you need looking after." I squeezed the hand that lay obediently in mine and smiled. "You're too nice."

"Oh, is that the problem?" asked Dad, smiling back. "We'd better look after each other, then."

"Deal."

The phone rang in the kitchen, and he leaped up as though he'd been expecting it. "That'll be Graham now. He said he'd call to settle some of the details."

He disappeared, shutting the door behind him. I was abruptly alone again. I got to my feet. I did not know what to do with the tenderness I had been feeling or how to stop the thought of Graham Cooke turning it sour. Except—I stepped to the window and felt the sun's kiss light on my forehead. Outside the lawn was streaked with light; bright beads of light hung on the leaves. That was enough. I needed to get out of the house.

4

House Calls

MEL'S PLACE LAY on the other side of town, on the busy road that ferried traffic north to the highway. The house itself was hidden behind a row of larches its builder had planted some thirty years before, when the road was hardly more than a lane for tractors. Now, as Dr. Gaspard complained, they needed all the help they could get to keep up the pretense that they had escaped from town to country. The back of the house was more convincing. A barn, a paddock, a reed-turreted stream, and then a sweep of fields and woods. In this setting only a rambling stone farmhouse would have looked right, and that was what had once stood on the site of the Gaspards' home. But the building had been left derelict, and in its place had risen a square block with central heating, French windows, and a terrace. Its walls were yellow stone, pocked with rustic chips of flint, and the name on the door was Beulah; but Mel's family called it the Sand Castle.

I dismounted and pushed the stiff white button on the front door. At length Lee Gaspard appeared.

"Mel? Oh, yeah, she's around the back, I think," he ventured when I asked.

"Listen, did I wake you up or something?" Lee seemed slightly dazed. He bent over me, as though he were trying to read something printed in small letters on the top of my head.

"What? No I was about to reach level ten of Star Quest, that's all."

"And you let yourself get zapped while diving for the front door. What a sacrifice!"

"No, no, don't worry, I paused the game," he said. "You can see it if you like." He ran his hand through his hair in a harassed way, and I tried to keep myself from following the specks of dislodged dandruff that powdered his shirt.

"Another time, maybe. Do you mind if I find Mel?"

I went through the living room and out onto the terrace. Mel was nowhere to be seen in the garden or the paddock, but I knew where to find her. I crossed the paddock toward a stone barn stranded in the field beyond. This was the oldest of the buildings the Gaspards had inherited with Beulah. They had converted the ground floor into stables for their two horses. The loft was officially a storeroom, but in fact Mel's unassailable domain. Here, on certain days, Mel would forego vivacity and curl herself on the broad sill above the wall heater to gaze back at the house, observing and unobserved. If I looked up now, I knew I would see her staring palely down, like some invalid child in a Victorian story.

I climbed the ladder to the barn loft. I loved the smells of hay and leather that filled this place and the dark corners where all kinds of equipment were kept, left over from when Beulah had been a real farm. Mel, at her station on the windowsill, was surveying the paddock. Her copper hair was spread across her shoulders, and she leaned upon her elbow in a way that suggested something fine and poetic. Beside her lay the Jane Austen novel we were meant to be reading for our exams. I saw with envy that she had nearly finished it.

"So you managed to feed your father all right?" Mel said without looking around. She made it sound as if Dad would probably have had to be burped.

"It's a long story," I said. "Do you still want to go riding?"

Mel stood up and slowly stretched, testing each limb. "Of course." Turning, she swept her hair back, put it into a ponytail, and became normal Mel. "I've been counting on you. My dear mother's been threatening to take me to the garden center."

"The garden center? What for?"

"I'm artistic director in this family, didn't you know? 'Melanie dear, you have such an eye for color, we really must plan our spring beds *together* this year.' Brrr! Come on, let's make our escape!"

We took our tack from the loft and groomed and saddled the two horses. Mel rode Hagar, a chestnut mare with a disposition like honey, who whinnied appreciatively in expectation of some illicit tidbit. Josh was different, a skittish, creamy white gelding. Josh made me nervous. Despite a childhood devoted to pony stories, I wasn't very experienced with real horses. They shared the paddock with an ancient donkey who had come with the house, and whom Mrs. Gaspard (rifling the Old Testament in search of a suitable name) had rechristened Enoch.

We left the paddock and followed the next field where it bordered the edge of the wood, until a metal gate revealed the entrance to a bridle path. Mel dismounted and led Hagar through. The sunshine of an hour before had dissolved, and I felt a sudden stiff breeze whip across my jacket.

"I suppose you realize my brother fancies you," said Mel unexpectedly as she remounted.

"What, the Zit King? Come off it. What makes you think that?"

"The way he was staring at you when you came out of the house. I can see straight into his room from the loft."

"You sure he wasn't staring *through* me? That would be more like him."

"Eyes like limpets, no kidding. You have an admirer, Petra. A doting beau."

"Well, I'm sensible of the honor," I began in my best Jane Austen voice, "and I know he's your brother, and no offense, but . . ." I caught Mel's eye. "You are joking, aren't you?"

"As if I would. Just don't be surprised if he invites you for a dirty weekend on Planet Betelgeuse one of these days."

I laughed.

"Remember the words of the prophet," Mel intoned, and put Hagar into a trot.

I watched her long ponytail bob up and down a few yards ahead and urged Josh to catch up. But he shied suddenly, and I found myself clinging to his neck. "Hey, easy!"

"What's the matter?" asked Mel, looking back.

"I don't know—it's Josh, perhaps he doesn't like this weather."

The weather was getting worse, it was true. The last patches of blue had been banished to the horizon, hastened by a chilling wind. The sky was a heap of gray-white ash.

We traced the margin of the field, grateful for the wood's protection.

"Century Hall, did you say?" asked Mel abruptly.

"What was that?"

"This morning, in town. You said Century Hall was on your paper route."

"I was there yesterday. What about it?"

"It's just that Dad dashed off there about an hour ago. It must have been some kind of emergency because I found his reading specs by the TV afterward. He never forgets them."

"Is Mr. Century ill?"

"Stands to reason, doesn't it? I don't suppose it's that old biddy who grabbed you this morning—she looked healthy enough to me."

"She didn't *grab* me," I corrected. "We just bumped into each other."

"Don't you believe it. You weren't looking, but I saw. It was about as subtle as Laurel and Hardy."

"If you say so," I murmured. I was picturing the scene in Century Hall. There lay Mr. Century, wrapped in his parcel of blankets. His possessions were ranged about him, each one charged with the past—a thousand little bombs of memory that only Mr. Century's mind could detonate. And in strode Dr. Gaspard, full of breezy bedside confidence. I saw the doctor wait impatiently for the thermometer, casting his gaze over the treasures congregated on the mantelpiece, tables, dresser—and a low alcove I hadn't noticed on my previous visit. Before, it had been hidden by a velvet curtain, but now the curtain was drawn to reveal a cluster of odd-shaped bottles with glass stoppers and, on a lower shelf, a curved tobacco pipe with a wooden bowl that—I *knew*—would fit as neatly into the palm as if it had been molded to it. A summer's day, a lawn, a long-awaited question—the smell of rosewood and cut tobacco flickered through my mind as I traced this thought back to its source and lost it in a tangle of smoke.

"Petra! Look at that!" said Mel, pointing at the field ahead.

A belt of wind was running like a wave through the long grass. It curled around the head of the field and came back down the slope toward us. Momentarily I stood in a breathless pocket of air, then the wind slapped into me, and Josh sprang forward, jerking the reins from my fingers.

"Here, let me take him." Mel's voice was nearly lost in the gale. But Josh staggered away, sideways and backward, trying to free himself from the invisible assault. Mel reached again for the loose reins, but again Josh pulled clear.

And he was bolting for the woods. I gave a shout as I saw the low branches swinging near and clung desperately to Josh's neck. No question of controlling him. All I could do was keep my head down, away from the hooked branches snatching at my hair. The earth churned up toward me, thrown out in clods. I closed my eyes and concentrated on keeping a grip on Josh's mane.

Josh left the woods but did not slacken. He was climbing all the time, first over grass, then up a clattering path of flagstones. When the echo of his hooves finally slowed, I found myself being carried toward a long, low wall. I took back the reins but still he would not obey, and when an arched gateway appeared I couldn't prevent him from entering.

We passed through an enclosure full of greenhouses. The

scent of weeds lay heavy on the air. Ragwort and cow parsley
pushed aside the broken glass, and from a trellis hung a tapestry
of creepers. I tried stroking Josh's neck to reassure him, but my
own hands were still shaking. He trotted on purposefully to
another gate. Through it, what had once been a lawn was planted
with apple trees.

And beyond that, through the trees' twisted branches, lay a
building that I knew. Its long walls hunched stiffly. The windows
were narrowed into points of stone, frozen in shock or disdain.
Its two wings pointed away now, for the building had its back to
me; but I recognized Century Hall as if it had been a person, and
its sullen stance characteristic of a mood.

Josh continued up the sloping lawn toward the Hall.
Whatever summons had brought him here still held him, and he
trotted past the apples where they lay, head forward and on
parade. At the back of the Hall ran a terrace with a stone
balustrade, each pillar crowned austerely with an urn. A
moment before we reached it, Josh turned away, toward the
Hall's ruined wing. He carried me down a narrow alleyway,
made narrower by the sycamores that sprouted there, and soon
I recognized the blackened stonework of the fire-damaged
rooms, seen from a new perspective. As we rounded the wing,
I caught glimpses of the courtyard, visible through the windows
of two walls, and the long interval of darkness between. The
courtyard was not empty, I realized. People were moving: there
was a flustered commotion, skittish horses, black plumes, the
hiss of fire and water. And voices: urgent, fearful voices. Josh
was going to carry me right into this confusion—

We turned into the yard—and at once the people and

horses fled. They leached into the shadows or slid away across the surface of the day. The turbulence collapsed into an echo, ringing in my ears. It was Century Hall itself that loomed above me, with no sign of human life at all.

I shivered. Josh was restless, too, shifting uneasily on the cobbles. The two abandoned wings stretched about me with their curious welcoming gesture.

I had been wrong—the yard was not empty after all. A small, fluttering figure was standing on the porch. It lifted its skirts and hurried across the cobbles toward me. As it ran the fluttering subsided, until by the time it reached me it had become Mrs. Campbell, her drab cardigan draped across her shoulders. She reached up and grabbed Josh's bridle.

"Thank goodness you've come! I knew you would, since he asked to see you. But you're too late, I fear."

"Mr. Century?" I asked, still in a daze. "Mr. Century? Is he ill?"

"Ill!" repeated Mrs. Campbell fervently, as though that answered everything. "His breath barely mists the glass!"

"He's not—" I couldn't bring myself to say the word in my mind. Mrs. Campbell might crumble to dust at its touch.

She looked at me blankly. "You must hurry! Even now there may still be time." She started to lead Josh across the courtyard.

I let myself be led. For a moment I thought that Mrs. Campbell must have mistaken me for someone else; but perhaps it was I who was mistaken. Since Josh had bolted, nothing seemed certain. Then Mel emerged from behind the burned wing, out of breath from riding. She must have been close behind the whole time. When she saw me and Josh, she leaned forward in her saddle and shook her head.

"I've never seen Josh do that before. Are you all right? You gave me an awful fright."

"We're okay," I said. I felt a wave of gratitude at Mel's appearance. The world, temporarily off balance, had swung back to its proper axis.

Mrs. Campbell's stream of protestations had not ceased. "He was well enough to take some soup this lunchtime. The bowl was empty when I found him, but he—poor man—was still as a stone. And the doctor fusses, but he's beyond that, far beyond . . ."

"Is my father here?" Mel interrupted. "Dr. Gaspard?"

"What can he do?" replied Mrs. Campbell. "When a body's worn so threadbare, you cannot hope to patch it. He said as much himself. Didn't even try to get him to the hospital. Said he might as well die under his own roof as take up one of their valuable beds. It may be five days, it may be five minutes. What does time matter, after all?" And with that bitter inquiry, she disappeared toward the porch.

"She wants me to see him," I explained.

"Then you'd better go," said Mel. "I'll come with you—I've never been in a haunted house before."

"Wait a moment. I haven't told you—"

Mel raised her hand. "We're wasting time, see?" She nodded to the porch, where Mrs. Campbell was waving at us to hurry. Mel started toward her.

"Oh Mel!" I sighed under my breath.

A minute later, I was walking into Century Hall, past the wavering mirrors and the dark wallpaper and the smoky light of the oil lamp. Mrs. Campbell kept up a muttered commentary, in a monotone that was too low to need any reply from Mel or me. She opened the door to Mr. Century's room, and a waft of hot, chamomile-scented air drifted past. We were about to go in when Dr. Gaspard emerged. He glanced at Mel and me, and although he said nothing, it was clear that he wasn't pleased to see us. He shut the door behind him.

"I've given him something to make him sleep more easily," he told Mrs. Campbell. "Remember what I said. If he becomes agitated again, call me. I can be here in ten minutes. In the meantime he needs rest and quiet—*no disturbances*." He began to put on his coat, which had been hanging over the back of a chair. "I think we'd better leave Mrs. Campbell to her work, hmm?" he said, turning Mel by the shoulder.

"Oh, they've been no trouble, doctor," said Mrs. Campbell hastily.

"Nevertheless . . ." Dr. Gaspard responded, but all the time he was guiding Mel and me toward the door. I for one was happy to go.

At the last moment Mrs. Campbell leaped forward unexpectedly and took my arm. "But you'll come again? You know he was asking for you? You'll come!"

I stared down at the lean hand on my sleeve.

"Come tomorrow! He so much wants to give you the last gift himself. It would mean so much."

"I think what Mr. Century needs more than anything else is rest," said Dr. Gaspard, gently removing her hand from my arm. "Rest and quiet, that's the way. I'll call again tomorrow. Goodbye, Mrs. Campbell." Somehow we had reached the door, and as he spoke he maneuvered Mel and me through it.

Once on the porch he turned on us. "And just what was *that* all about?" The bedside manner had definitely gone. "Have you no sense at all? Following me like that on an emergency call. What did you think you were playing at?"

"We weren't following you," retorted Mel. "It was Josh—he ran out of control and ended up here. Petra got carried through that wood at the top of Sherman's Hill. He just . . . stopped here."

"It's true, Dr. Gaspard."

"And Josh persuaded you to go and disturb one of my patients? A frail old man? Don't you realize how irresponsible that is?"

"But that woman invited us in!"

"Mrs. Campbell is old, confused, and in a very understandable state of distress. You, evidently, are not. I'd have thought that by now you would have learned—Oh, never mind!" He made a dismissive gesture. "I'm going to get the car. I'll see you at home."

Mel stood looking after him. "Well, what do you know?" she said quietly. She was angry, too, but in a way that would not show itself, not just yet.

"We caught him by surprise, that's all," I said. "You can see how it looked."

She shook the mood from her shoulders. "Oh, don't worry about him," she said. "He's going through a *stage,* you know." She walked across the courtyard to see to Hagar.

Josh was standing on the cobbles beside the stable door. I wanted to tell Mel what I had seen through the windows of the burned wing, but after this business with Dr. Gaspard it would have to wait. I unwound Josh's rein from the bolt where I had tied it, and he nuzzled his head into the warmth of my coat.

"So you expect me to be friends, after the fright you gave me?" I ran my finger down the long white bridge of his nose. Josh looked back at me, his eyes innocent. "Oh, all right, I know what you want. Not that you deserve it." Digging into my coat pocket, I felt for the dusty bar of chocolate I kept reserved for Josh.

"Ow!" I sucked my forefinger.

"What's the matter?" asked Mel, already mounted.

I felt inside the pocket and produced a silver earring. "I just jabbed my finger."

Mel reached down to take it. "Pretty," she said. The earring draped itself over her finger, the stud balanced by some kind of fruit hanging on a short chain. "A pomegranate, isn't it? Who gave you this, then? Don't tell me Lee has a secret rival!"

"I've never seen it before! I don't know how it got there, honestly."

Mel arched an eyebrow. "Really! Well, you're a one for secrets, aren't you, Petra?" She studied the earring speculatively before handing it back. "Long life, rebirth, *fecundity*—oh yes, especially that, I'd say."

"What are you talking about?" I was wary of Mel in this mood. This new object was baffling enough without her trying to be mysterious. Could someone really have meant it as a gift?

"I can see you've never read *The Secret Language of Fruit.* These things have hidden meanings, you know. You should hear my mother on the subject —she could squeeze a novel out of a decent-sized window box. Yes, pomegranates are as fecund as they come."

"All right, I give up. What does 'fecund' mean?"

Mel smiled infuriatingly. "Well, Petra, if you have to ask, you're obviously too young to know."

"Which means you don't know either," I said. I was ten months older than Mel, but it didn't seem much of an argument.

"Look it up," said Mel, and walked Hagar to the far side of the yard. I was annoyed to find I couldn't tell whether she was bluffing.

I retrieved the chocolate and let Josh take it from my open palm. "Fecund, indeed!" His warm breath enveloped me as if it were some intimate secret we were sharing, a secret in which Mel could have no part. Then I hoisted myself back into the saddle and turned to the curtained windows beside the porch. I almost expected to see them twitching shut. The last few moments had been haunted by another presence, and I wondered if I was being watched. But the eyes of Century Hall stared back, stone blind.

No doubt Mrs. Campbell was seeing to Mr. Century, stoking the fire or adjusting the tuck of a blanket. No doubt our visit had long since been chased from her harried mind; and no doubt, too, the appearance of the earring in my coat had nothing to do (but now I suddenly thought that it might) with our collision that morning, on a half-deserted pavement in the mist.

I clicked my tongue in the way I had learned from Mrs. Gaspard and was pleased to find Josh for once responding as he should. We passed around the far end of the burned wing, and this time its darkness held nothing more than a flaking mass of charred rafters.

"Come on, Joshua," I said, and Josh broke into a willing trot at the touch of my heel. He carried me back across the lawn and through the apple trees, past the ungathered harvest lying there.

5

La Primavera

BACK HOME, Dad had worked a transformation. The chilly hall I had left earlier that day was gone, along with the dingy shadows that had filled it—banished by a new orange bulb. The stereo had been coaxed back into life, too: I found I was taking off my coat to the accompaniment of Frank Sinatra. The speakers still faded in and out, but that was more than made up for by Dad, who was upstairs serenading his shaving mirror.

"These vagabond shoes . . . are longing to stray . . ."

All this, *and* two bars on the fire—the kind of extravagance that would have earned Jamie a lecture on Money and the Real World. I flopped onto the sofa, glad to feel the warmth stealing back into my hands after the bike ride from Mel's place. My fingers were red and numb—as if someone had replaced them with a row of rubber carrots as a practical joke.

"There you are—I was beginning to wonder." Dad appeared at the door. He had a towel around his neck.

"I was only over at Mel's. What time is it, then?"

"Don't worry, I'm not nagging. I ordered a taxi for seven P.M., that's all."

"Where are you going?"

"Not me—us. We're having a meal out tonight, to celebrate my new job. La Primavera. Italian is your favorite, isn't it?"

"La Primavera! Can we afford that?" I asked automatically, then wished I hadn't. He was clearly making a grand gesture.

"You sound more like your mother every day," he laughed. "Yes, we can afford it for once—and we deserve it, too. You've got to mark big occasions, you know."

"What about Jamie? Is he coming?"

"Jamie's staying the night with Babushka. Seems he really has come down with the flu, poor chap. She didn't want to risk it. Don't worry, you can imagine the fuss she'll make of him."

"Mmm," I agreed, imagining just that. "Still, it's a pity he has to miss out."

"There'll be other opportunities. You forget, I'm one of the employed now. Look, it's twenty to—you'd better get changed. They don't allow jeans in La Primavera."

I showered and changed as quickly as I could, digging out the nearest thing I had to a smart dress—a short black number that Mum had once pleased me (though she had not meant to) by calling "slinky." Then I took the silver earring from my coat pocket. Mel was right, it was pretty, but its appearance still bothered me. Could Mrs. Campbell really have slipped it there? And why—to spook me? She had more important things to do. Besides, I refused to be spooked—I would wear it instead. A dab of toothpaste shone it up nicely: the pomegranate tapped against my neck when I moved. It felt comfortable there, as if I had always owned it.

By the time I got downstairs, Dad was beginning to fidget.

"Are you ready?" he asked, unable to suppress a glance at his watch.

"I'm starving, if that's what you mean."

Through the frosted glass of the front door, we saw a car's headlights draw to a halt, then hover expectantly. "There's timing! Come on—no, ladies first. We might as well get used to doing things properly. They're very particular at La Primavera."

Later, outside the restaurant, he paid the taxi driver with a flourish, overdoing the tip as usual. We stepped through the drizzle to a pair of smoked-glass doors, where a white-jacketed waiter came forward to take our coats.

"Table for two, the name's McCoy."

"If you'll follow me," said another waiter, who had been leaning back against the bar. He was sleek and handsome, casually arrogant in the way he looked us up and down—the sort of man Mel spent much of her time trying to meet. As we walked to the table, I glimpsed our reflections in a mirrored pillar: the waiter, gliding like a swan through a lake of deep blue tablecloths, followed by me and my father. Dad was handsome, too, I decided—surprised it had never occurred to me to think of him that way. Distinguished, yes, that was the word, with his well-groomed mustache, weathered face, and the streaks of iron in his hair. He was actually better looking now than when Mum had been alive. A strange favor, that, for grief to have done him.

Our table was in a large alcove, lit by a candle floating in a china gondola. By my place stood a tiny vase of flowers and a napkin folded cleverly in the shape of a scallop. I eased myself in, almost falling back as the waiter surprised me by helping me with my chair.

"Well then, Petra, what do you think?" Dad asked when we were alone.

"I've never seen so much cutlery! Are we going to eat this meal or take out its appendix?"

"Don't show your ignorance!" Dad scoffed. "You're not planning to show me up in front of quality, are you, lass?" he added in his Yorkshire voice.

"Of course not—never fret," I assured him. It was a favorite expression of Mum's, and he caught the inflection.

"Nay lass, I'll not fret," he said. Even so, I was not the person he would have liked to have been taking to dinner that night. In a way I was standing in, as always.

The restaurant was filling slowly: it was still too early for the night crowd. Dad leaned forward confidentially. "I hate to say it of my own flesh and blood, but I'm not sorry Jamie isn't here tonight. We'd never have got him to come to a place like this."

"Not unless they did chips, no. Will he be all right with Gran?"

"Babushka? Of course he will. The question is, will she be all right with him?"

"I suppose that's what I meant!"

"Oh, she loves to fuss. I know she doesn't like to show it, but beneath that tough exterior, there's an old dear with bifocals and a ball of knitting. She'll be glad of the excuse."

I smiled to think of my gran with knitting. At seventy-three she still thought of herself as much too young to be a grandmother and would take any opportunity to recount how many lengths of the local pool she had swum that morning. Babushka—that was Dad's nickname for her—would have risen in indignation at the suggestion she knew the difference between knit and purl.

The waiter came to take our order, and I was impressed to see how expertly Dad pronounced the names of the wine and food, with just the right concession to an Italian accent. I had certainly never thought of him as cosmopolitan. In fact I had never even been to a restaurant with him—not a *proper* restaurant, where the waiters didn't wear cardboard caps or wipe the table with a cloth as you left. Perhaps my parents had been here when Jamie and I were small, or else in that mysterious existence they had enjoyed before we were born. There was so much of their lives I hadn't even been curious about until recently.

"We came here once," Dad told me. "Soon after it opened. Your mum loved Italian food, just like you."

"I'd forgotten."

"Oh yes, and she could speak the language, too, up to a point. I remember she tried to strike up a conversation with one of the waiters, asking which part of Italy he came from, and so on. All the stuff out of her phrase book. Of course, it turned out he was from Liverpool! Couldn't understand a word she was saying. He only put on an accent to impress the customers."

"What a poser!"

"He'd probably been told to do it. Helps the atmosphere, like the mandolins and the Botticellis on the wall. There's no end to the things people will do just to earn a crust."

"I hope you remember that when you're working for Graham Cooke."

Dad looked wounded. "Thank you, Petra. I trust we're not

going to have remarks like that all evening."

"No, sorry," I said. "I promise I won't mention him again. And I won't eat peas with my knife, and I won't talk Italian to the waiters. All right?"

"Right. Ah, here's your chance to behave. Mine's the tagliatelle."

We were still being served when we were distracted by a disturbance at the door. Someone was talking above the mandolin music, arguing with a waiter who was trying to direct him to the back of the restaurant. Then an insistent figure in a dark coat paced toward our table.

"So you made it after all! Well done, Dick. And good evening to *you*, Petra."

Dad looked startled, but only for a moment. Graham Cooke was talking again. "I see you've ordered without us—well, I can't blame you for that. I've had the tagliatelle here myself on occasion. I'll just go and help Sarah with her coat. Waiter—can we have two more settings at this table, please?" And without waiting for a reply he returned to his companion.

"What's *he* doing here?" I hissed as soon as he was out of earshot. Then I added with suspicion, "Did you know he was coming?"

"Of course not!" protested Dad. "I mean—I'm as surprised as you are."

"He didn't seem surprised to find *us*."

Dad looked uncomfortable. "I suppose he might have said something about dropping by. You know, the way people say these things without really meaning them. I certainly never expected—"

"It was going to be a special night—for us!"

"It still is! It still can be."

"Not if he's here. Dad, tell him to go away. Tell him it's a family dinner—he can't just barge in."

Dad winced. "You know I can't do that."

"Why not?"

"Petra, you know why not. Just be patient, will you?"

Graham Cooke was returning now, accompanied by a slim woman of about thirty. Even I had to admit she was beautiful.

"This is cozy, isn't it?" said Graham cheerfully as he sat down. "We'll have to watch our elbows. Dick, I'd like you to meet Sarah Thrale."

"Pleased to meet you." The woman smiled and inclined her head in a way I thought unnecessarily regal.

"Sarah works in television," Graham added.

"Only local television. Graham, you mustn't make it sound grander than it is," scolded Sarah Thrale. She put her hand on Dad's arm and explained: "Graham has this idea that we spend all our free time being photographed going in and out of nightclubs."

"*That's* where I've seen you before!" Dad cried. "You present *South in Focus.*"

"You've seen it?"

"Of course! That is, I'm afraid we watch you with our dinners on our knees," he added, and this time it was my turn to wince.

"I wouldn't worry about that. You'd be surprised, the things people do in front of the telly." Sarah stole a private glance at Graham. "So you're Richard McCoy—Graham's told me a lot about you."

"All good, before you ask," chimed in Graham through a mouthful of garlic bread that he had carelessly reached over to take from a basket beside my plate.

"And this is your daughter?" She glanced in my direction, and from the way her gaze slid over me, I saw I'd been relegated to the kindergarten.

"This is Petra," explained Dad. He hadn't noticed that Sarah's tone would have been better suited to a six-year-old. In fact he made it worse by adding, "She's just started her half-term holiday."

"I can speak for myself, you know!"

There was a moment's silence. Several of the other diners looked over. I hadn't meant to shout, but that was how it had come out.

"So it would seem," Sarah Thrale laughed.

"Now, Petra, don't start," Dad began. But it was too late.

"We weren't really expecting company tonight, Mr. Cooke." I spoke quietly, in an effort to be dignified. "It was going to be a private celebration, just family."

"Ah, but we're *old* friends, aren't we, Petra?" said Graham, winking at me as though he were a favorite uncle.

"That's why you should understand. We just want to have some time together to celebrate Dad's new job."

"Of course you do. But then, since I'm the one who gave him this new job," said Graham Cooke, "you could say I'm the founder of the feast." He took another piece of garlic bread and popped it in his mouth. "Couldn't you?"

"That's not the point!"

"No? What do you say, Dick?" Graham's voice was casual

enough, but his eyes did not leave my father.

Dad tested each word carefully, as if they might not be able to take his weight. "I'm sorry, Graham. I think perhaps this wasn't such a good idea . . ."

"Don't worry," interrupted Sarah Thrale brightly. She had been looking more and more uncomfortable. "There must have been a silly misunderstanding here. It would be just like Graham to get the wrong end of the stick. I don't believe he listens to *me* half the time."

Graham Cooke was still looking at Dad. "Yes," he said at last, "perhaps we'd better leave you to it. We were thinking of going for Thai tonight anyway, weren't we, Sarah? And they do seem to have squeezed you into a corner. Here, you don't mind if I just— this is *very* good." He stood up and leaned across the table to take the last morsel of garlic bread. As he bent down, his head passed near me, just an inch from my face. Above his collar the spongy skin glistened slightly. It had an odor—I remembered it now, from the old days—of musky aftershave, sticky as a fog . . .

I lashed out, catching my tonic glass with my knuckle. The glass fell to the carpet and smashed, spilling its contents over Graham's suit on the way.

"It's all right." Sarah Thrale hastened to dab at Graham's thigh with a napkin. "It's only water, it won't stain . . ."

"Can I be of any assistance?" offered the waiter, appearing like a genie.

The couple at the nearest table looked over curiously. The man made a comment, at which his partner gave a barely muffled laugh. Graham Cooke had snatched the napkin from Sarah and stalked off to the men's room. Dad looked around helplessly, hoping to find some magic button that would rerun the last few minutes with different results. I sat gasping in my chair. And the mandolin tape looped around again and began the same old love song.

The taxi dropped us on the pavement outside the house. This time Dad did not overtip the driver.

"He didn't seem to mind too much," I said. I was trying to revive a conversation that had already ground to a halt earlier in the car.

"He did mind. He was just too polite to show it. Not something anyone could accuse *you* of. Honestly, Petra, what got hold of you? I've never seen you like that." Now we were home he sounded more shocked than angry.

"It was seeing *him* again, so suddenly."

"I know you don't like him, but that's no excuse to drown the man."

"I didn't mean to! I felt ill—it was an accident." The words were just words. I couldn't bring myself to care if he believed them.

"You were well enough a minute before." He fumbled with his key, getting it stuck in the lock as usual. "Blast this thing!"

I made us both sandwiches and mugs of sweet tea. It didn't seem much compensation for a meal at La Primavera. "I'm sorry, Dad. I didn't mean to spoil everything."

"It was on the way to being spoiled in any case." He sat at the table with his cheeks cupped in his hands and the jacket of his suit riding up at the shoulders. I knew this mood of his—too close to my own for comfort. The truce was over, and the tortuous descent to bad temper had started again. Nothing good would get said tonight.

He stared for a time at the sandwiches, then lifted the top of one cautiously, as if he suspected it might be booby-trapped. "Salami!"

"Well, we did want to eat Italian, didn't we?"

He laughed despite himself. "Not quite what I had in mind!"

I put my arm on his shoulder. "There'll be other times. You said so yourself."

It was the wrong move. He turned in his seat and looked me full in the face. "You really don't understand, do you? I could lose my job over this."

"Graham Cooke's not going to sack you because of an accident with a glass of tonic water!"

"Isn't he? You don't know him like I do."

"I know him well enough! And he knows when he's on to a good thing."

"Meaning what?"

"Meaning you're a good draftsman, of course!"

"Meaning I'm a dupe!"

He turned back to his sandwich, took a bite, and pushed it away. "You're not as grown up as you think you are."

There was only one direction this conversation could go, and I didn't have the energy to follow it there. "I'm going to bed. I feel like I haven't slept in years."

He nodded but did not raise his head as I left the room. Then he called after me, like someone remembering a chore: "Tomorrow. We'll have to talk."

I called down the stairwell: "There's really nothing to say."

I'd reached the landing before I felt his eyes on my back. I turned to find him standing in the hall below. It was strange how far away he looked, how small and sad, with his jacket hanging loose and his face drooping like a balloon that's had some of the air let out. Good-bye, I thought. As if the stairwell was an ocean, and I was drifting across it to a new life: Good-bye, good-bye forever. I wanted to say something to reassure him, to tell him I still loved him, but the words sat sourly on my tongue.

For a long time I lay with the bedside light on, neither asleep nor awake. Thoughts billowed up like smoke, and I watched to see the shapes they would make—the shapes of Dad and Graham Cooke, or one, or both, or neither. Mrs. Campbell was there too, hands clasped in a desperate plea; but I was watching another person, in a silent melodrama of years ago.

The pomegranate earring was tap-tapping against my neck. I had forgotten to take it off when I undressed. Wearily I raised myself on my elbow and fiddled with the catch. The mirror on the dressing table showed me in reverse, black hair falling about my head. So small, the figure on that bed, in the white night-gown. I had always been tiny, they said—pearl-small and moon-pale. I turned out the light and pulled the sheets up close. I was excited about something but could not remember what. I sighed . . . If only Edmund and father would be friends. They *would* be friends: I should make them. Then we should all be happy. Oh dear. If only I didn't feel afraid. Oh dear.

What time was it?

I had just woken. Remnants of the dream lay about me—a dream in which my room had been different and drowsy with flowers. *I* had been different. And now things were the same again. Up on the ceiling, the Darkling looked familiar, its wide mouth muttering spells. "Darkling," I said, and searched for the charm to protect me. But for once I could not find it. And when I listened, the Darkling's words were not the usual Darkling words, made of wind and splashing water. Tonight there was another voice. I twisted the sheet tighter in my hand and tried not to breathe. Perhaps it was just a trick of the wind. The wind could play some mean tricks, I knew, rushing through the walnut tree's thin branches. But in the lull that followed, the voice came again, and I knew I was being called.

"Eurydice."

6

In the House of Love and Cinnamon

JAMIE WAS IN A WHITE-PAINTED ROOM, with foaming seascapes on the wall. A washbasin, a collection of cream-colored jugs, and a pile of thick towels on a wooden chair were all set flush against the wall, but next to them came a conspicuous gap, the size and shape of a pine chest. The chest itself now stood at the end of Jamie's bed (the rucks in the carpet showed that dragging it had been no easy task) and was home to a portable TV.

"I've brought you some grapes," I announced, placing the bag on his bedside table. "It is the seedless ones you like, isn't it?"

"That's right," said Jamie weakly. After a moment's consideration he added, "I'd rather have ice cream, though. With chocolate chips."

"'Thank you, Petra, how thoughtful of you.' Honestly, Gran, I thought people were meant to go all saintly when they were ill."

"Jamie's been very good," said Babushka, judiciously. "On the whole."

I laid my hand on Jamie's forehead. "He's still got a temperature."

"Enough to keep him here for a while," agreed Babushka. "Tell your father it's no trouble, by the way. I've had more practice at this than he has. Besides, it sounds as if he's going to have his work cut out with this new job."

"And Jamie doesn't mind? You don't mind stopping here for a day or two, do you?"

"Of course I don't. Gran's got cable."

"That's all right then!"

"*And* she knows how to cook, and she doesn't shout at you all the time. Beats home any day."

Looking around the room, I could see Jamie's point. The remote control lay in easy reach on the pillow, close to his computer game. In addition, Babushka had gathered an impressive collection of comics, scattered casually on the bed. From somewhere amongst them the face of my pampered brother peered out wanly.

After lunch I helped Babushka cook the last apples from her garden, a wilderness of Bramleys and gnarled cider trees. We carried the fruit up from the cellar, where she had sorted and stored it in crates weeks before, and piled it on the kitchen floor. The apples mushed slowly in a huge copper kettle, filling the house with the sugared scent of cinnamon. Babushka prided herself on self-sufficiency and even sold her surplus applesauce to the local delicatessen, complete with printed labels. While she peeled and cored, I stirred the kettle, enjoying the monotony. It was nice not to have to take responsibility for a while, almost like being a little girl again. Helping Mum in the kitchen.

After a night of bad dreams, the day had started with a sullen breakfast. Dad and I had carefully avoided all mention of

Graham Cooke, and as a result had spent most of the time in silence. The atmosphere had improved only with a phone call from Graham himself. Graham was full of understanding. He made a joke of the restaurant—it was nothing, an accident that could have happened to anyone. Dad had been relieved, of course; but I saw that even now he wouldn't be able to let the matter rest. I could feel his sidelong glances probing me from the corner of the room. I knew what would follow. First the little tests: Graham's name dropped into the conversation like a stone into a well, with a long silence before the splash. And then the questions, all so kindly meant ("The last thing he wanted was to see me unhappy"). But why couldn't Graham and I just be friends? Dissolve old memories in a handshake and a smile? For Dad perhaps that was possible, but for me some memories would not dissolve. Some were too sharp for comfort.

Better to be cooking apples in Babushka's kitchen.

"Careful, it'll burn," said Babushka, returning from the garden with an empty peeling bucket. I'd left the gas on too high, and the mixture was starting to turn to caramel.

"Sorry, I was miles away. Is it ruined?"

"I think we'll salvage something." Babushka peered dubiously into the kettle. "You've done enough stirring, anyway. I'll tell you what, you go through to the sitting room and I'll make us some tea."

Gratefully I relinquished the kettle. "That sounds perfect."

Babushka ushered me through, then disappeared again. Occasionally I glimpsed her ferrying kettle and mugs to and fro. I watched her lazily. White hair . . . red sweatshirt . . . navy blue leggings. A tricolor being slowly waved.

"You seem a bit thoughtful today," Babushka called, as the kettle clicked itself off.

I jerked awake. "I do?"

"Is it boy trouble?"

"No, Gran, not exactly," I replied with a sigh.

How typical, homing in on *that*.

I looked along the shelf above Babushka's desk. It was filled with romantic novels, all of them written by Babushka herself. She had taken to writing as a hobby when she retired and had soon discovered a talent for matching spirited blonds with scowling heroes, in a variety of historical settings. Now she produced one or two books a year, tapping them out on a word processor to the accompaniment of Rachmaninoff and Tchaikovsky. Often the mail would bring fan letters from as far away as America: in a quiet way, she was a success. "Thank heaven for bored housewives," said Babushka cynically when she received these letters, but anyone could see she was flattered. Not surprising, perhaps, that she should use a grandmother's privilege to speculate about my boyfriends. I was getting to an age where they'd begun to be noticeable by their absence.

I took down the nearest book. It had the usual picture of a perfect couple, this time in Regency dress. They clutched each other passionately, while behind them a white mansion burned to the ground. A few daubs of soot on the woman's face suggested a narrow escape. The man's eyes were in shadow, but the flames lit a handsome and vaguely sinister profile, the chin jutting clear of an elaborate cravat. Across the cover was printed *Plucked from the Burning: A Mary McCoy Romance*.

"Oh, put that away," said Babushka as she came in with a tray.

"You would have to pick up the worst thing I ever wrote."

"It looks very steamy, Gran."

"Well, that is the object of the exercise," she replied with dignity. "Within limits, of course."

I took a sip of the scented tea. "Shades of Century Hall," I said experimentally. The picture of the burning house had reminded me of something I'd meant to ask. "Do you remember the fire up there? It must have been exciting."

"Ah, is that it?" Babushka looked surprised, but at the same time as if she had suddenly solved a mystery. "Yes, your dad did mention you'd met old Mr. Century."

"I was on my paper route—he invited me in. Gran, that place can't have changed a bit in eighty years. It was creepy. *He* was creepy."

"But he gave you a present, your dad said." There was a note of rebuke in her reply. Apparently this entitled Mr. Century to more respect.

"A book of poems."

"Well, that was really very generous of him. What a strange man! Last of the great eccentrics."

I stared into my cup. "I suppose so."

"A dying breed. You won't meet many of his sort."

"I don't expect I will," I said without regret. I hadn't meant the conversation to take this turn. Dying breeds were a kind of protected species—you weren't allowed to snipe at them. "But why should he give it to *me?*" I exclaimed. "He doesn't even know me!"

"Why shouldn't he?" said Babushka. "That's the sort of thing eccentrics do. I heard about a millionaire who left all his money to the man who checked his oil at the garage. And—well, probably Mr. Century doesn't have many people to be generous to."

"It wasn't like that. He wasn't being generous. The way he talked—it was more like he was trying to frighten me."

"Frighten you!" Babushka flicked the idea aside. "I don't suppose he was for a minute." But she added in a different tone, "Old people sometimes get wrapped up in their own private worlds, that's all. Especially if they're ill and alone, they tend to live more in the past. I've noticed it myself. Memories come to seem more real than the here and now. No wonder if Mr. Century behaves strangely after all these years. His hasn't been a very happy life, I imagine. And he must be *so* old."

"One hundred and one," I reported dutifully.

"That much! Yes, he would have to be."

"He's ill, too. At death's door, from what his housekeeper said."

"Well, there you are. No wonder you're upset, poor love." Again she seemed relieved to have pinned the problem down so neatly.

"I'm not upset!" I said, with a bit too much vehemence.

"Death is always upsetting," Babushka insisted. She peered at me through the thick glass of her spectacles, trying to gauge the exact measure of my upsetness. She was thinking of my mother, I could tell. "But it's worse when it comes unexpectedly. When you get to Mr. Century's age I don't suppose it holds many terrors. Perhaps he even feels ready to go."

Or perhaps not, I thought. Mr. Century had looked set to cling to life down to the last bloodied nail. *That* was what appalled me—I had it now.

Jamie's voice sounded from upstairs. *"Graaan!"*

Babushka was already halfway to the door. "Here we go— soft-drink patrol. You stay there, I won't be a minute. He's probably feeling left out." I sat back into the chair from which I had half risen. I had the feeling that in Babushka's eyes I was hardly less of an invalid than Jamie himself. Did I *look* incapable of fetching my brother a drink? In the mirror opposite my eyes were sparking coals, my face as pale as ash. Smoky hair. Dream-haunted. I leaned across the table and took a Coke, remembering what I'd learned about blood sugar levels.

Dad must have told Babushka about La Primavera, I decided. She had been warned in advance, recruited to find out what was the matter—that was it. Nothing else could explain that dogged look of concern. They'd gone behind my back. I felt subtly betrayed at that, as if my unhappiness were no one's concern but my own.

On her return, though, Babushka's thoughts were elsewhere.

"What a fusser that boy is! He wants his bed remade every five minutes. I pity his wife, when the time comes."

"Jamie's not getting married," I corrected her. "He's made up his mind. He's going to live alone in a trailer and travel the world."

"We'll see how long that lasts. He'll be quite handsome, you can tell. He's got his father's face, underneath the puppy fat."

"Don't tell him that, Gran! He already thinks he's God's gift."

"He'll find out soon enough, if I'm right. They say women are vain, but give men half a chance, and . . . Well, your Mr. Century was another one."

"What? Another what?"

"Handsome, I mean. Quite a heartthrob."

"It's true, then? He really was good looking?"

"Oh, it's true. When I was a little girl, I often used to see him riding through the village on horseback—the very model of a dashing ex-army officer. And then of course he was a Century, which automatically made him the most eligible bachelor in the neighborhood. I think a few hearts fluttered for him in those days."

I smiled. It was hard to connect this splendid figure with the husk of a man I had met. Though I'd always vaguely known of this other Mr. Century, for the last few days they had inhabited my imagination separately, linked only by a name. Could time alone really work such a transformation? I attempted to conjure the younger man, but could get no further than a chocolate-box figure, tall and slim on a moonlit terrace, with silver shadows playing across his face. Piano music drifted from the room behind him, and his head nodded slightly in time to it. Then he paused to draw from a pipe with a swan-necked stem. . . .

"He never married, did he?" I asked quietly. That moonlit picture had been infected with sadness.

"No he didn't. He was engaged, of course, to the woman who died. On the night before their wedding, too! But I've told you that old story?"

"Not since I was small. I was too young to understand it then."

Babushka could take a hint. "It was all of sixty years ago, of course. But a place like Cooper's Bridge has little enough romance, so we know how to make it last." She glanced at the row of novels over her desk. "They were cousins, I believe: Edmund Century and Eurydice Tremain."

"Eurydice?" I was listening now.

"She was a daughter of the rector over in Tellerton. I know that, because our neighbor was a maid there at the time. They were brought up just a mile or two apart, I suppose. Although Eurydice was much younger than our Mr. Century. She'd have been no more than a child when his army regiment was posted to India. I don't suppose he'd have looked at her twice in those days. But by the time he came back, after he inherited the Hall—well, ten years make a difference. The new Eurydice was beautiful. I remember her very well, a tiny creature with jet black hair and a face as white as the moon. Small enough to hide in a pea pod, but perfect. Any man might have loved her, but as for Edmund Century, it was as if he'd fallen under a spell. From the moment he saw her, he could think of nothing else. He was obsessed. That was the kind of love it was."

"Gran, this could be one of your books!"

"My books have happy endings," said Babushka gravely. "Edmund had changed too, of course. They say he'd got a taste for the mystical, traveling in the East. Karma, reincarnation— exotic philosophies for this part of the world. But he was always an eccentric. Perhaps that's why he courted Eurydice the way he did. He'd been used to ordering men about, but she made him as shy as a schoolboy. Anonymous poems or gifts appearing out of nowhere, anything but speak to her face-to-face. Once—I'll never forget—our neighbor went to clean Eurydice's room and found it filled from top to bottom with lilies, bunches and bunches of them. And all the beams hung with honeysuckle. The scent! I've no idea how he managed to spirit them there. Poor Eurydice must have found it all rather bewildering. But in the end they became engaged"—Babushka paused to curl her legs up onto the sofa—"and I suppose they thought they would live happily ever after."

"But?" I asked. Of course there had to be a *but*.

"There was trouble about the wedding, I remember. In those days a wedding at the Hall was a big occasion. But Mr. Century surprised everyone again—he refused point-blank to be married in church. He had his own plans. You see, ever since he'd come back to England, he'd been busy putting the Hall to rights. In one of the wings was a little pagan chapel he wanted to renovate—the Temple of Pythagoras. One of those architectural fancies the gentry used to indulge in when they had more money than sense. Mr. Century was going to restore it to its original glory."

"I didn't see it," I said.

"There's a reason for that. Mr. Century wanted a civil wedding followed by a ceremony inside the temple itself. He'd even worked out his own version of the marriage service. Incense, temple bells, that kind of thing. Eurydice's parents were not amused. They said they'd refuse their consent if Mr. Century didn't get married respectably—which for them meant in church, with a clergyman and choir and *Hymns Ancient and Modern*. In the end he seemed to back down. But then, the night before the wedding, there was a dinner party at Century Hall. He and Eurydice took a romantic moonlit stroll. The next thing anyone knew, Mr. Century had burst into the drawing room, shouting like a madman. There'd been an accident, a fire in the temple, and Eurydice was trapped. Everyone rushed to help, but by the time they found Eurydice, she was dead. Quite unburned, I understand. She'd sheltered in a cavity under a stone altar, where the flames couldn't reach her. I suppose she'd suffocated from the smoke. The inquest said death by misadventure, but I know Eurydice's family never forgave Edmund Century for what happened."

I hesitated. "They didn't think he'd killed her, did they?"

"Who knows what they thought? No, not deliberately perhaps. But it seems he'd persuaded her to go through a kind of marriage ceremony with him after all, alone in the temple. A mystical union of their souls, according to rites of his own invention. That meant fire and sacrifice and bloodcurdling oaths, if you believed the stories going around the village afterward. Anyway, something went wrong. A lamp set light to a hanging and trapped them inside. Mr. Century escaped, but Eurydice was too frightened, and then the fire became fiercer and it was impossible to get out. The Tremains held Mr. Century responsible for leaving her there. Perhaps he did himself. I know he never went to her funeral at Tellerton. He was ill with remorse, people said. And after all, he's put himself in prison ever since." Babushka stopped and poured herself another cup of tea, as if with that sixty-year-old accident, Mr. Century's history had come to an end.

"With Mrs. Campbell as his jailer," I prompted.

"Who?"

"Mrs. Campbell—his housekeeper."

"Oh yes! I'd forgotten all about her. She's one of those people who seems to have been there forever, isn't she?"

"And then some," I agreed. I found myself remembering Mrs. Campbell's tiny form as it ran across the cobbles to greet me the afternoon before. The shawl-like cardigan flickered in and out of the autumn wind like a gray flame. Then the Hall loomed up, and against its walls the flitting gray of Mrs. Campbell was lost to a shadow on the stonework.

"All the same," I added, as I stared into my cup, "if you weren't looking at her, I don't believe she'd be there at all."

7

The Legend of Zelmar

BY THE TIME I JUMPED OFF the bus in Cooper's Bridge High Street, I was the only passenger. The driver grunted, the doors folded shut, and the bus shuddered off up the long hill toward the Composers' Estate. The last mile to our house, coming from Babushka's, was always on foot. Black and gray clouds skimmed the roofs ready to rain at random, but just now the pavement shone dishwasher fresh. It was quiet in a Sunday way, but quiet was not what I wanted. I wanted music, and lights, and people, and a sharp thudding beat I could feel in the pit of my stomach. I wanted to visit the Music Cellar.

Most shops in Coopers Bridge are shut on Sunday, but the Music Cellar is always full of kids playing the consoles or looking at CDs they can't afford. There's nothing else to do, unless you like slumping on a sofa all day. That's where Dad would be, most likely. I didn't want to go home yet, not to that. Not while I was still thinking about Eurydice Tremain. I turned into the Music Cellar and went down the stone steps, past walls plastered with two-tone posters. The music I could hear from the street was hip-hop, but by the time I reached the basement shop it had changed to a slow ballad, and the half-dozen customers were moving past each other in a kind of murky waltz. I settled at the *W*'s, studying each disc by seven colored lights.

"Death is always upsetting," Babushka had said—meaning Mr. Century. But it was not his death she had told me about, it was Eurydice's. And it was Eurydice's name I had heard the previous night. I supposed I had known the story before, somehow—from when Babushka had told it to me as a child. And it had chosen just this time to bubble up through all those years of silted memory and take the shape of a nightmare. That was why I'd heard her name and dreamed all night of fire and soiled water. I turned the disc over, checked to be sure the plastic sleeve was really empty. Kidding myself.

The manager bustled up beside me. "Can I help you?" she asked, but helping me was clearly not her life's ambition. She was in her fifties, with a hard face full of angles. Too old for this kind of job.

"I haven't decided whether to buy anything yet," I mumbled, and examined the disc I was holding as if I was interested in it.

"Let somebody know when you're ready, won't you?"

"All right, I'm putting it back. Okay?"

"There's a young man in the next room, just the same," she said with a seen-it-all-before sigh. "He's been camped in there since lunchtime. He's not with you, is he?"

"No, he's not." I turned in a dignified way to leave the shop, but then two girls lurched in with hair sopping, and I decided to forget dignity and wait out the rain with the computer games next door.

She must have been wrong about the young man. No one

here was more than Jamie's age, and most of them were in little competitive gangs, huddled over computer screens. Good. I edged to the far corner, hoping to be left alone.

"What are you doing here, Petra McCoy?"

Lee Gaspard appeared like a jack-in-the-box from behind a low case of glossy books. He had a paperback in his hand and a finger tucked in to keep his place. The rest of his body seemed at a loss, as usual. His elbows were flapping dangerously close to a large cardboard cutout of Sonic the Hedgehog.

"I'm looking at the games, of course."

"But that's not your thing, is it? Besides, all you've done is stand there looking shifty." He lowered his voice. "You're not hiding from someone are you?"

"Of course not!" I snapped. The question irritated me, somehow. "You're the shifty one—the woman out there said so. I wouldn't be surprised if she's calling the cops right now."

He looked so shocked I had to reassure him. "Only joking, Lee! You take everything seriously, don't you?"

"Do I?" replied Lee. "I'm sorry."

"There you go again!"

"Perhaps I'm just a serious person." He squeezed past a pair of blond boys with sugary spikes for hair. From the expression on his face, it looked as if he was considering letting me in on a dreadful secret. "I've been copying stuff out of this hint book, that's all. It's not really ethical."

"Ethical" was typical Lee. It didn't sound like the sort of thing you'd land in prison for. "What hint book?"

"*The Legend of Zelmar.* I've been stuck on it for weeks—wandering around a lot of forest glades. If I don't get out soon, I'll die of thirst or hunger. Unless the troll gets me first."

It was one of his stupid games, of course. I should have guessed—Mel had told me all about them. Lee's day wasn't complete if he hadn't killed a wizard or rescued a kingdom from certain destruction—all on the computer, naturally. There's always some stupid prophecy, and a missing talisman, and the hero doesn't know who he is because his parents (the King and Queen) have given him away to be brought up by a woodcutter.

"First I need to bribe the gardener to lend me his trowel, so I can plant the bean," Lee explained. I wondered if the rain had stopped yet. "I'm already carrying the bean, of course. It was lying at the side of my plate back in my humble cottage."

Was I looking at all interested? I didn't mean to, but that didn't stop Lee.

"Once it's planted, I've got to water it, so of course I need chewing gum to mend the bucket at the well."

"Of course. What else would you use?"

"The book says I should find some stuck under the table at the tavern—if I can avoid losing it in a fight. And then with luck the beanstalk will grow, and I can climb up to the next Scroll. Simple."

Throughout this he had been standing over me, with that slight stoop that made me afraid he might topple over at any moment. "Isn't it cheating, though—to look all that up in a book?" I said, stepping back slightly. "Cheats never prosper."

"I bought the game, so I get to make the rules. Think of it as research."

"You didn't buy the book, though."

"That's true, I didn't buy the book." He agreed as if it hadn't been a criticism. "You still haven't said what you're doing here. Is Mel with you?"

"No, she's not. I am allowed out on my own, you know—now I've learned to tie my laces."

Lee laughed nervously. "I didn't mean it to come out like that. Who needs a reason? This place is a refugee camp on Sundays. Sooner or later all the outcasts from suburbia wash up here." He shook his head in mock concern at the glowing faces of the younger boys. "Another doomed generation," he announced with relish.

I moved to the other side of the room, pretending to be interested in a game some boys were playing there. A man in a space suit was striding down a metal corridor, flamethrower in hand. Now and then an alien would attack him from behind, or he'd hop over a land mine. Lee followed me, attached by an invisible string. I kept thinking about what Mel had said: "Eyes like limpets."

I turned to face him, so abruptly he nearly walked into me. I'd never seen him this edgy. "Aren't you getting a bit old for video games? Look at all these other kids. Most of them still believe in the tooth fairy. And you're what, seventeen?"

"Eighteen, nearly," he nodded, then added with a weird smile, "That's when I leave off games and take to drink."

"Oh, terrific!"

"Or maybe I won't. Maybe I'll stay this age. Getting old's for losers, anyway."

I gave up. It was as if he was spouting nonsense just to keep the conversation going. One thing was certain, Lee wasn't cut out to be a twenty-first-century Peter Pan. Adolescence had him firmly in its grip—a volcanic landscape of zits had seen to that. "I got it wrong, it's *you* who believes in the tooth fairy."

"I'm trusting to science, cryogenic suspension or something. They've proved that aging is just a genetic malfunction. I'll be in the freezer till they sort it out, then . . . Everlasting Lee! They'd better hurry, though, I can almost feel myself becoming a responsible adult day by day."

I watched the space-suited man explode on the screen in front of me. Immediately he flickered back into life and resumed his task of incineration. When I looked again, I found Lee grinning at me, a foolish expression on his face.

"What are *you* staring at?"

"I was thinking of buying a chocolate shake," he replied in a voice that was meant to sound casual. "That place behind the bus station is open. Want to come?"

So that was it. All this time he'd been building his nerve to ask that question. That nonsense about cryogenic suspension and *The Legend of Zelmar* was just a way of putting it off, or working up to it, or—worse!—showing off for my benefit.

It still took me by surprise, though. I looked down at my watch, wishing I'd had more practice at what I'd got to do now. Lee was nice enough, after all: he'd just never quite got the knack of being human. But half an hour of elves and orcs across a formica tabletop was more than I could stand. "Sorry, I'm on a diet," I said rather quickly, and tried to mix a smile in with my shrug. "Maybe another time, eh?"

That seemed a bit offhand, but there was nothing more to say, was there? Lee followed me from the shop anyway—the invisible string was holding up well under the strain. It was raining hard, and I stopped under the awning to zip my coat.

"Well, 'bye then," said Lee, no longer playing it cool but shuffling awkwardly from foot to foot. I decided I preferred him this way. It seemed to come more naturally.

"See ya." I was occupied in unsticking my zipper.

Lee did not move. He looked as if he had more to say. What did he think this was, *Brief Encounter*? I tugged again at the zipper, determined not to look up. Then he seemed to change his mind and turned to cross the street.

"Watch out!" I yanked him back by the arm. A van sped past, blasting on its horn. The wash from the tires soaked us both to the waist. The van disappeared, horn still blaring, and we were left with the tap of rain against the awning.

"Thanks," said Lee, dazed. "I wasn't looking where I was going."

"I know that!" I shouted furiously. "You had your eyes too well glued on me—Zit King!" The words just leaped out. I couldn't stop them.

Poor Lee stepped back in astonishment. He looked as if I'd socked him in the face. "Come on! It was nothing. No bones broken, see?"

"You should look where you're going!" I hissed.

"Next time I will, okay? Why the panic?"

I stared at him, raindrops bouncing off hot skin. "Because I've seen it happen before, that's why!"

"I don't understand—"

"That's how my mum got killed, idiot. All right?"

A couple emerged from the Music Cellar behind us, both in jeans and jean jackets. I recognized the girl from school—a junior, big in the Drama Society. "Lovers' tiff," she commented, in a whisper that was meant to be heard.

Lee had his hands in his coat pockets and his elbows tucked into his sides, like a badly folded deck chair. "I'd forgotten."

I leaned my head against the wall and wished I was somewhere else. My breathing seemed very loud. "It's not your fault," I said. "I'm sorry, I shouldn't have shouted at you."

"Do you want to talk about it?" Lee offered. "That shake's still on offer. Or maybe you're shaken enough?"

"Ha-ha. No, I'd better get home. I'm expected."

"Then I'll walk you as far as the Common."

"*Walk* me?" I sniffed, rainwater dribbling down my face. "I'm not a poodle, you know!" I set off toward the Common, toward The Rise and home. By the time I glanced back, Lee was no longer to be seen.

8

The Darkling

DAD LOOKED UP from his work. "Hello, Petra!"

He unbent from the drawing board and turned to me in his swivel chair. The desk lamp behind his head scattered a flock of shadows. "I didn't hear you come in."

"You were lost to the world."

I came down the concrete steps into the workshop and picked my way around the hollow chassis to where Dad sat marooned in an island of yellow light. Beside him stood an old filing cabinet, flecked with white paint from ancient decorating jobs. Its drawers hung open, and from most, long rolls of paper lolled down. Others contained the tools of his meticulous trade—set squares, rules, protractors, and other instruments whose names I've never known. Though not an organized man, in this one part of his life he could transform himself into a precise and patient craftsman. He would stand, or sit, or hunch at the paper for hours at a time, humming under his breath: so careful, so slow, until a miraculous structure stood revealed, knitted by a thousand joints and sinews. Then, months or sometimes years later, he would take me to see the building that had grown in imitation of his drawing, proud as if his labor had con-jured every brick.

"What are you working on?"

"Something Graham brought round. He's only been in busi-ness a week, and already he's got a rush job on. Say what you like about that man, he doesn't let the grass grow under his feet."

I would not rise to that bait. "So you've been at it all day?"

"Apart from listening to Ted Deakin. He was nattering on about the fireworks. I had to agree to help out again—it was the only way to get rid of him."

"Come on, you know you love it."

I peered over his shoulder. The desk lamp showed a sparse network of lines, in which the outline of a door was the only recognizable feature. Most of Dad's efforts seemed to have been devoted, not to this abstract landscape, but to a series of cartoon figures populating the margins of the paper.

"Oh, you remembered the Petroids!" I cried.

"It wouldn't do to leave them out. Who's going to get this thing built?"

All around the edge of the paper were tiny sketches of me, engaged in a series of tasks. Petra driving a bulldozer, Petra up a ladder, Petra with a clipboard, directing operations with a wag-ging finger. The Petroids. When I was small, Dad had always drawn them to decorate any job he was working on. He had made a game of pretending it was the Petroids who oversaw each project: they were like elves in hard hats. Years ago I had squealed with delight; now I was surprised he even remembered them. Unlike me, the Petroids had not grown. They were stuck at five or six years old, with pudgy cherubic faces.

"We've had a lot of visitors for a Sunday," Dad remarked. "That Mrs. Campbell was here not half an hour ago."

I managed to make my voice sound quite unconcerned as I replied: "Oh? And what did she have to say for herself?"

"That's what's so odd—she didn't say anything."

"She just stood there?"

"By the time I got to the door, she was already gone. Well, you know I have the radio on sometimes, so perhaps I didn't hear the bell right away, but I don't think that was it. I could just see her at the end of the road, and she was beetling off as if she'd planted a bomb. First time I've seen someone skulking at twenty miles an hour."

"You sure it was her?"

"She left a note with the box. Didn't you notice it when you came in?" Dad nodded toward a small cardboard box lying on the workshop steps. "She must have carried it all the way down from Century Hall—it's drenched right through. I'll be surprised if she doesn't get pneumonia herself."

I went to examine it. The waterlogged cardboard sagged through my fingers, and I was aware of something smooth and heavy inside.

We took the box into the kitchen. I laid it on the table, beside the orphaned fragments of car engine. A long string had been tied around it, but the cardboard fell apart almost before we could cut it free. Inside was a mass of paper, apparently meant for wadding. I plunged my hand in and felt it close about an object slightly larger than my fist.

It was a bottle, creamy white. It might have been made of glass, but if so it was a kind I had never seen. There was a waxen quality to it that made me think it might take a print from my fingers. I held it to the light and dimly saw the syrupy movement of liquid, reaching nearly to the squat glass stopper.

"I think I've seen this before," I said.

But Dad wasn't listening. "I almost forgot—here's the note that came with it." He took a slip of paper from the wall heater, where it had already dried to an ancient crinkliness. "You don't see copperplate like that much these days. They really knew how to teach handwriting when Mrs. Campbell was at school."

> *I know you will take this gift, since it is in the nature of a bequest. Mr. Century died peacefully at six o'clock yesterday evening, God rest him! Before the end, he asked me to give you this. It was hers once, and it will be a remembrance, the third and last. He saw you had a pliant soul.*
>
> *Forgive my haste, but I have a great many arrangements to make, and little time.*
>
> *Hester Campbell*

"Poor old chap," commented Dad, who had wandered around the table to look over my shoulder. "You obviously made quite an impression."

But I had had enough of Century Hall. "I don't want it. Throw it out. I don't want anything more from him."

"You can't do that, not with a gift. It wouldn't be right." He picked up the bottle and examined it. "It's a scent bottle, isn't it? Quite an old one, too." He reached to take the stopper from the bottle.

The stopper leaped out in his hand, with a sound like an exhalation.

"Hmm, do I detect a hint of jasmine?" he asked, in the voice he had used to order wine the evening before. "Or perhaps—Oh, that's disgusting!"

He slammed the stopper back. "It's *foul*. Like something died in there—rotting away."

"Here, let me." I took the bottle and pulled at the stopper. The glass molded itself to my hand but would not move. "It's stuck. What did you do to it?"

"Nothing! Why do you want it anyway? You were right, Petra—chuck it in the trash bin. You don't want rancid stuff like that around the house."

I fingered the stopper, noticing only now that it was decorated, with knotted patterns of leaves and flowers pressed about its sides. It reminded me of something—of the flower pattern on Mum's jewelry box upstairs. Slowly the stopper eased itself into my palm.

"No, you were right." I tilted the bottle, and the sluggish liquid gleamed with a faint rainbow haze. "It *is* a gift."

My gaze slid down from the bedroom ceiling, along the lilac-patterned wall, and came to rest on the dressing table. Eurydice's bottle and book sat where I had laid them earlier. Her silver earring, too. That had been Mr. Century's second gift, I realized—with Mrs. Campbell once again his messenger. Though why he wanted it to be mine I still could not guess. Next came more familiar silhouettes: my hairbrush, a painted clog Dad had brought back from Amsterdam, and on the corner the little jewel casket that had been my mum's. The casket lid was open wide.

I closed my eyes.

We had been out shopping. It had been late summer, and I had needed shoes for school. A hot, resentful day. Dragging along pavements, hanging back at every shopwindow. Finally I had heard Mum call my name for the third time; then, "Very well madam, you'll walk home." In the window's reflection I had just been able to see her spin on her heel and step off the pavement. Then there was a thud. No scream, no squeal of brakes— there had not been time for either. The whole street had held its breath, conspiring in a moment's silence. Even then I must have hung back; by the time I reached the place, there was already a small crowd. I had had to fight my way through—I had actually kicked my way through the knot of bodies to the place where my mother lay.

I shifted on the pillow. What came next? Oh yes, the sirens, the arm around my shoulder, the lights and disinfectant smell. There was a policewoman with me, her hair tied back so tight it must have hurt. *My name's Michelle.* I hadn't thought the police used first names on duty. But those were the only words I remembered from that hour: *My name's Michelle.* Surely it would be against the rules, like drinking? Then Dad had come to the hospital, still with a stub of pencil behind his ear. They had given me something to make me woozy and put me to bed. This bed. And as I fell asleep, there was the sound of a bell, and slamming doors and voices, and the dim knowledge—growing dimmer and darker and seeping into all my dim, dark dreams—that half my world had simply . . . ever so simply . . .

"No one ever really dies. How often you have wished that could be true!"

It was the Darkling who had spoken.

I froze. Gradually I opened my eyes and looked up at the ceiling where the Darkling's face formed each evening, a nightly coincidence of light and shadows. There was nothing to see. It was a collection of branches quivering in the wind outside, that was all. A childhood bogey. Nothing. My familiar objects were lying about me, armchair, hi-fi, all ordinary and comforting. Except they were not comforting anymore.

"No one truly dies," the Darkling repeated. "Each of us is eternal. Only the form changes."

The voice was fluting, imperious, schoolmasterish. It was Mr. Century's voice, as Mr. Century might have sounded in the days when he rode his horse through Cooper's Bridge.

I moved my tongue to speak—but even to speak felt like giving in to a thing that had no right to be happening at all. "Who's there?"

"Who's there?" A gust beyond the window shook the trees and convulsed the Darkling's face in goblin laughter. A different, deeper voice answered softly, "Man or woman, young or old, alive or dead. Who would you wish me to be?"

Downstairs I could hear an orchestra swoon with delight at the final clinch of hero and heroine. Dad was watching an old movie on the VCR.

"You're not real! You're just a made-up creature!"

"Then make me real, make me new! That godlike power is yours. Imprint me with yourself. It is not such a leap to make, for two creatures as lonely as we are."

The Darkling's voice was lost in a spatter of rain against the windowpane. At the same time the scent bottle on my dressing table had changed: it seemed to be glowing with a cool light of its own. Unwillingly I looked toward it. The light from the bottle flickered, as though it had been disturbed by someone walking close by. The bottle was moving, melting. It was forming shapes: a leaf, an insect, a dog, a horse. And then human faces, each held for an instant. One after another they melted and set, until the bottle found a fixed expression, which was my own. The solemn face was captured looking slightly down, eyelids hovering on the brink of sleep. I knew the likeness was perfect, but the longer I stared the more it seemed alien, the face of a stranger.

The Darkling spoke, a snaking voice that curled about the feet of every word: "We all have many faces, many names. Why should death be the end, my love? It is the casting of a skin, that is all. Or the falling of a leaf—but the tree survives, the tree flourishes! The body that was mine has fallen away, old and spent. Now no impediment remains. You invited me, and I have come. Rejoice in the true marriage of our souls!"

"I didn't invite you!" I gasped.

"You will not deny it," insisted the voice. "Are my thoughts not your thoughts? My memories your memories? Are we not already nearly one? You *must* admit me." The voice slithered into the corners of the room.

"You're not even real!" I'd never been so scared. But the Darkling was an illusion—I had to hold on to that.

"One of us is not real—but which?" asked the Darkling with a sudden craftiness. "Which is it? Perhaps I imagined you, many years ago."

"You're just a lot of shadows from the garden," I croaked. "If the streetlight went out, you wouldn't even exist."

"Unfair, unfair. We are all invisible in the dark. But I am like you—*I can speak for myself, you know!*"

That was the worst of all. It was my voice, my own words, just as I had shouted them in the restaurant. The last bulwark of certainty shuddered and gave way. I felt myself beginning to melt under the gaze of the face on the dressing table. I was no longer sure where I began or ended. Looking down at my hand, I saw only a pattern of wind-cast light.

"Let me in," whispered the Darkling, this time with the wheedling entreaty of a small child. "You must, you must, you must."

"No!" I replied. But a cloud was rising around me. The edges of my room, the familiar ceiling jigsaw of plaster cracks, grew dim. Only the Darkling remained, and my own waxen image floating like a specter.

"You *must* let me in. It is a sleep, that is all, a slow, soft falling."

"No, please, no." But the memories fell from me like leaves. I was being stripped, like a tree in winter. Voices came, whispered voices, and now a voice at my shoulder: "Never fret, love. Never fret." My hand was clasped. A half-forgotten touch shot through me. Then that, too, was caught in the stream and spun away into blankness.

"Come back!" I called.

"Feel the years melt away from between us!" cried the Darkling. "Time itself is standing aside. Soon we shall touch. Soon love will unite us forever."

"I don't love you!" I screamed. "I hate you!"

For the first time the Darkling faltered. The mist seemed to quiver and buckle. When the voice returned, it was old Mr. Century's, in a senile whisper. "Eurydice? You promised me. You must not desert me, after all those lonely years."

But I had heard its weakness. "I'm not Eurydice. I never promised anything. This is *my* room!"

"You're wrong!" exclaimed the Darkling, but its certainty had vanished, and I knew that I was right. The mist was thinning. My bedroom loomed up as it dispersed.

"You've no right to be here. Leave me alone."

"You took my gifts! You opened the bottle!" cried the Darkling in outrage. "Without you, I'll be left all alone. My heart will break!" It gasped, finding it hard to breathe. "Remember the lilies! The moonlight on the lake! Oh, I miss you so . . ."

Immediately I did remember—a sultry night long ago, with tender voices and oars feathering the water. But they were another person's memories. "I wasn't there," I said.

There was a sound of sighing, as if someone were straining every muscle and finding it too much effort. Then came the crash of glass above me. The Darkling split into a mask of fragmentary lines. It filled the whole room—its bony face was everywhere, thin fingers scrabbling at my throat. And the wind! The wind pinned my arms and spattered me with years of rain.

"Lie still! Lie still!"

There was a shape beside the door. It slid like a phantom toward me.

"Don't try to move, Petra. Are you hurt? I heard you scream."

"Dad? Is that you?"

"Don't move, love. Let me get the light."

He stepped away, and a moment later the light switch was clicked on and off, several times. The room was still dark. Fresh rain blew in through the shattered window.

"Must've taken out a power line," he muttered. His face hung dimly over me, through the maze of intricate and leafless branches. Mustached moon-face, staring at me . . .

I began to laugh. I couldn't stop myself.

"There's something lying on me," I giggled.

"It's the walnut tree from the garden. Petra, what a fright for you! Looks like you've got half of it in the bed. You're not hurt, are you? It's my own fault, I should've chopped it down years ago, but—"

"Dad, can you get me out?"

"Yes, yes of course," said Dad, stumbling over his words. "Look, I'll need to get some light. Do you know where the flash-light is?"

"Dad?"

"Under the stairs, I expect. That's where it used to be."

"Dad? Don't leave me."

"I'll only be gone a moment. I've got to find a light."

I heard him take the stairs two at a time down to the hall, and I smoothed my finger over a long slither of glass lying by my right hand. The spasm of laughter was over. My arm was beginning to throb badly. I had not felt the pain at all at first, but now a dull ache was growing into something more savage.

Downstairs a noisily metallic object fell crashing to the ground—possibly the pile of paint cans just inside the cupboard door. Curses followed, then a kind of muffled rummaging, until at last Dad reappeared with a paraffin lamp swinging from a hoop.

"Wouldn't you know it, the battery in the flashlight was leaking. But I found this old thing."

He set the lamp on the dressing table, where it sent the bottle's shadow stalking across every wall. A bough from the tree outside was still leaning in at the window. Another lay broken-backed across my bed. Dad bent the smaller branches back and carefully lifted them.

"Can you slide out?"

I squirmed under the branches, shielding my eyes with my good arm. The floor seemed farther down than I remembered.

"There you are—free at last!"

"Thanks, Dad." I was surprised to hear my voice sound so normal. I didn't *feel* normal at all. "I'll be all right now."

"Look, I've brought some plastic sheeting from the workshop—I'd better start shutting the rain out. Sleep in Jamie's room tonight, love." He shook his head. "What a mess! I'm not looking forward to seeing this little lot by daylight. You are all right, aren't you?"

"A bit shaky," I admitted.

"Of course you are."

I took my bathrobe from the back of the door and eased my arm into it, biting back a hiss of pain. Dad was already tapping a nail into the window frame, while the polyethylene sheet he had brought with him flapped about his head. "Is there anything I can do? Holding the sheet in place, or something?"

He turned to me and lisped through the clutch of nails in his mouth: "Go to bed!"

9

History Revision

"**RENAISSANCE SHEEP!** They're what did the damage." Mel snapped her fingers.

"Huh. Just as I suspected. Sheep, yes?" I tried to sound knowledgeable, but I didn't know what she was talking about.

It must have shown. "Enclosures! Rich men fencing in the common land for grazing. All the people who'd been farming there for generations had to leave. Then they became vagabonds and were arrested for *that!*"

"That's a shame. That's shameful."

"But true. Write this down. 'In 1608 five hundred acres of common land to the north of Cooper's Bridge were enclosed and turned over to pasture by Sir Thomas Malkington. Despite the opposition of the local—'"

"Sir Thomas who?"

Mel put the book down and shook her head reprovingly. "I sometimes wonder if you've done any work toward this project, Petra. I don't carry passengers, you know."

"Sorry. Not awake yet."

She leaned down from the bed and turned the tape around.

"Well, nothing's going to make local history interesting."

In the paddock outside, Enoch stood motionless. He might have been a pile of stones. If I sat still long enough, perhaps I would become part of the landscape, too, then I wouldn't have to take my exams. Studying with Mel was worth it of course— her name alone was worth an extra grade in the eyes of Mr. Eldridge, our doting history teacher—but it could be very exhausting.

The music started, a deep American voice supported by a swerving bass line.

"Not that again!" I pleaded.

"I thought you liked the Welfare Cheats!"

"I do! Just not all the time, thanks."

Mel took the pair of dark glasses hanging from her breast pocket and slipped them on. "Is it true people begin to resemble their music collections?" With her eyes hidden behind the circles of impenetrable glass, she sucked her cheeks into an imitation of Bo Jansenn's death-row stare.

"I can't concentrate with this going on." I reached over to the OFF switch.

"No, I want to listen. Don't!" Mel knocked my arm away.

It was unexpected, and I flinched before I could stop myself. "Now what's the matter? I hardly touched you."

"Nothing. Go on, lust after Bo if you have to." The pain in my arm sang louder than the Welfare Cheats.

"Just this song, then we'll have some Nat King Cole, or whatever it is you like."

"Not me, my dad!"

"You're as bad as each other. Fancy saying *Casablanca* was

your favorite video the other week. In front of everyone, too. So uncool."

That had been a bad move, all right—especially when the teacher had agreed with me. I tried to change the subject. "We don't have a VCR at all at the moment, or a TV. I suppose that's about as uncool as you can get. You sure you still want to speak to me?"

Mel frowned. "There can't be any trouble with the rental now your dad's working?"

"The power's off, that's all." I told her about the storm. "We're squatting in our own house for today. Lucky the stove's gas."

Mel seemed envious. "I wish something like that would happen around here. It's so *boring!*"

"Yeah, well, Dad's enjoying it anyway."

This was true. The power cut had awoken Dad's spirit of adventure. Breakfast that morning had been spent reliving childhood exploits at his uncle's farm in Ireland ("*They* got by without electricity, gas, or piped-in water and raised three strapping sons into the bargain!").

Not that I took much of it in. I was still stunned from the night before. It was hard to believe—but I had won. For days I'd been expecting some disaster to jump me from behind, ever since that first meeting with Mr. Century. And the disaster had shown itself. The Darkling had tried to take me over, eating away at my memories like a worm in an apple—but I had overruled it; I'd faced it down. The Darkling was gone. Mr. Century was gone. I had, really and truly, won.

So why did I feel as if a shadow had just fallen across my path?

"This is one for you," said Mel, back in her history book. "More about the Century family. Your friend had some charming relatives, I must say. 'Sir William Century, botanist and founder member of the Royal Society, cleared several farms between Century Hall and Cooper's Bridge to create an area of parkland, where he bred many exotic species for the first time in England. His collection of Alpine plants is now in the possession of the Natural History Museum. The influence of his friend Sir Christopher Wren is said to be visible in the cupola of the Temple of Pythagoras, shown in the photograph opposite.' Well, that's changed a bit!"

She handed me the book, open at a glossy black-and-white print. I looked at it reluctantly. Although I was trying to think of Century Hall as just another heap of historical stones, that was a trick I couldn't quite bring off yet.

The Hall faced the camera head-on. The two wings funneled the gaze toward the blackness of the central porch. Slightly to the side stood an elderly couple, and next to them a tall man holding a white horse by its bridle. Through the grainy fog of years, the outlines of Mr. Century's face stared back at me. But now he was young and dashing, just as Babushka had described, in an officer's jacket and long riding boots. It was too far away to see his expression, but I thought I knew it. Aristocratic, with a sly challenge in the tilt of the head, that was his style.

Century Hall, 1920. Mr. Henry Century stands with his wife, Maria, and his son, Edmund. The Hall has been in the Century family since shortly after the Reformation. Note particularly the dome and spire of the Temple of Pythagoras, situated in the West Wing. This was the work of the botanist Sir William Theophrastus Century

(1629–1715), notorious in his day for his work on alchemy and the occult. Sadly, part of the Hall has since been damaged by fire.

The burnt wing, still intact, filled the left of the picture. Halfway along it was a square tower with a gilded dome, topped with a tall triangular spire. At the peak of this, precariously perched, two metal hoops joined to make a giant eye. So this was the Temple of Pythagoras—the place where Eurydice had died. Except that, for the people in the photograph, her death still lay in the future. I had a sudden impulse to warn them. Could I shake Mr. Century out of his complacent pose for the camera? Could I make him hear? He stared back—his head cocked, but not to listen. Too many years lay between us.

Mel put her chin on my shoulder. "You know, I was dreading this project. But a few more examples and we'll have the whole thing wrapped up. What about the villages out in the east of the county? We haven't got anything from Tellerton way yet."

"Good idea," I said, but I didn't move.

"It should be in the next chapter. Oh, give me the book— you really are half asleep, aren't you?"

Mel leaned down over me from the bed. Again she knocked my arm; and this time I couldn't stop a yelp of pain. The book fell to the floor. "What's wrong?"

"Nothing," I said, annoyed with myself.

"Did I hurt you?"

"It's nothing!" I snapped. "Just a bruise."

"A bruise?" Mel slid off the bed. In an instant she had assumed the brisk medical manner of her father. "Come on, I won't hurt you." She eased back my sleeve.

Along the length of my forearm, spaced at even intervals, were four livid bruises, with a fifth blistering in the crook of my elbow.

I felt like I'd been discovered naked. Mel stared and stared. She seemed to stare new holes into my skin.

"Where did these come from?" she asked finally. Her voice was different, quiet.

"I told you—about the accident last night. One of the branches came down on my arm."

Silence from Mel.

"It really hurt."

"Perhaps my dad ought to see this," she said. "It looks like it could go septic."

"Don't fuss. I'll be okay, I promise."

Mel still seemed uncertain. I'd never seen her at a loss for words before. "There's nothing you want to tell me? You know you can trust me, if—"

"What's to tell?"

"I'm not stupid, Petra. These look as if someone has . . . No, don't pull your arm away." She gazed at me. "Did someone do this to you?"

At first the words didn't make any sense at all. Then I saw it. I saw the suspicion she didn't quite have the courage to put into words.

"What are you trying to say?" Mel wouldn't meet my eye. "You're talking about my dad, aren't you?" It was so ridiculous, I felt like laughing. "He wouldn't hurt me in a million years!"

"All right, Petra." Mel was embarrassed. "You can see I had to ask."

"He's never laid a hand on me in my life!" My voice sounded high and squeaky, like one of those hysterical women in the films who get slapped in the face and then say, "Thanks, I needed that."

"I'm glad to hear it. I didn't mean to upset you. I take back every word, okay?" She let go of my hand at last. "Only, you were so touchy."

I drew the sleeve back. "If you knew him, you wouldn't have thought it for a moment." I smiled to myself, but my eyes were weepy and I kept them looking down at my arm where it lay in my lap. My mouth went on speaking of its own accord. "I think he's the gentlest man I've ever known. Too gentle, sometimes. He spoils Jamie and me. Do you know what he reminds me of?"

"Tell me," said Mel. *She* was too gentle—humoring me.

"One of those circus elephants, the sort that give little kids rides on their back. I mean, you know they could squash them without trying, but they're so careful, as if they'd rather die than—"

I was jabbering. Mel waited till I ran out of words and flopped onto the floor beside me. "So long as you know," she said.

"Know what?"

"That you could trust me."

"Of course I know."

"And there isn't anything else the matter? Now?"

"There isn't," I said. "There was, but it's sorted out. It's okay."

"You want to talk about it?"

I thought about it, I really did. I thought about taking all the pieces of the last few days and carefully sticking them into shape for Mel's benefit. The dreams that weren't dreams, the gifts that weren't really gifts, the memories that belonged in someone else's head. And the other things, like Graham Cooke and Dad's new job, things that weren't part of it but had got entangled anyway, the way they always do, so you can never peel a neat fact off from your life and hand it over, because there are fifteen other facts hooked on like burrs.

No, no, no. What did it amount to, this nest of ragged nightmares? And what would Mel prescribe for an inflamed imagination—cold showers? Like when I kept crying in class after Mum died, and my geography teacher had me levered into one of her character-building field trips to take my mind off it. Three days of storm-force winds on a sand spit in the Solent had been meant to cheer me up. But all I got were chilblains and an ammonite for Jamie's collection.

I picked the book off the floor and found Tellerton in the index.

"Like I said, it's sorted out. But I would tell you, Mel, I really would. If there was anything to tell."

10

Home Away from Home

Now I should tell you why I changed my mind.

By the time I got home, the walnut tree was already cut down, lying in the grass beside the house. There was a hole in the lawn where the roots had brought up a patch of ground, and a couple of plants were defying gravity to grow at an angle of ninety degrees. The garden was larger and lighter. Things that had been hidden for years were visible again—like the hedge of brambles by the fence, still with a few shriveled blackberries the birds had missed. And what was left of the herb garden. Mum loved her herb garden best of all, even though the plants there weren't much to look at, not compared with the flowers she planted on the roadside border, with reds and blues and yellows competing through the summer heat. Those flowers were running wild now. For the last two years they'd been left to get on without her, like the rest of us.

The walnut branches were piled beside the wall. Some had snapped off when the tree fell, but others had been sawed off, and stacked, and even smoothed down as if they weren't genuine wood at all, but just the kind of real-fire-effect logs you see in gas showrooms. I was impressed, I suppose. It wasn't like Dad to get a garden job done so quickly.

The living-room window opened above my head, and Dad's face peered out.

"Petra, come inside. I want you to see something."

I jumped back. "What are you doing here so soon? I thought you'd still be at work." It was only four o'clock.

"Never mind that. I told you to come inside." The face disappeared, and the window shut with a thud that shook one or two flakes of paint from the frame.

Maybe I was just surprised to see him there, but I didn't like that clip to his voice. That wasn't Dad. I mean, it *was* Dad, but it was odd, too. The way your voice sounds when you hear it back on tape, all strange and hollow. I let myself in and immediately banged my knee against something metal concealed in the shadows of the hallway. It took a moment before I recognized it as our electric fire. A fine stone dust coated my tongue. Cautiously I tried the door.

The living-room had been turned upside down. The TV was gone—unless that awkward bulge behind the curtain was it. The dining table had been dragged out from its usual spot beside the window, and both the flaps raised, as if we were expecting company. But we weren't expecting company—we hadn't eaten off that table in years. Dad sat in the low-slung wicker chair nobody ever used, the one that filled the gap (and hid the damp) in the corner. There was a gap-toothed hole where the fireplace ought to be.

"What do you think?" he asked, turning to me. He had the look of a cat who's dropped a dead sparrow on the mat.

"I don't know what to think." The fireplace was a mess, dust and bricks everywhere.

"That's not like you. You're the one who's always preaching the virtues of an open fire. Well, I decided you were right. A nice, wood-burning hearth for the winter. Of course, when this house was built that's what would have been here. I only need to knock out the brick facing. I've always felt *cold* here." He gave a shiver as he said it.

I took a step into the room. "Couldn't we have talked about it first?"

"What was there to talk about? I knew you'd approve. What better time than now, while the electricity's off?"

"*Still?*"

"Oh, we'll be all right," he said encouragingly. "Course, I'll need to get the chimney lining checked—"

"When will they put the power back on?"

"They're looking into it. You know what it's like. Bureaucracy . . ." He flourished the word like a charm. "Think of it as an adventure. We can make our own entertainment, like in the days before television. You know, charades and hymns around the piano."

"But we haven't got a piano!"

"We'll improvise!" He raised himself out of the wicker chair, which creaked complainingly as he pushed down on its arms. "There's always chess. I found that set you used to have, with the pieces shaped like silent movie stars. Remember?"

"I remember." Douglas Fairbanks was the white king, and all the pawns were Keystone Kops. He must have been going through my cupboards to finds that chess set again. I hadn't used it since I taught Jamie to play. (In those days I'd let Jamie beat me, just to encourage him. Which was fine, till one day I decided to play for real, and he *still* won. Somewhere along the line he'd passed me, and I hadn't even noticed!) Chess, indeed. I thought of the last set I'd seen, somewhere in the recent past. A chess set made of ivory, with gems for eyes, glinting under the light of a roaring fire.

A roaring fire . . . and no electricity.

I began to see the other ways the living room had changed. Different mementos on the walls and windowsills. Photos of me or Mum or Jamie, or of other people unknown to me, in uniforms, stiff posed smiles. Postcards from holidays years back. A sprig of lucky heather—all magpie scraps of the past. Somewhere in my mind a spark of fear flickered.

Dad stepped away from the fireplace. The dust in his hair had matted it with gray, like an old man's. After the first bout of enthusiasm, he was suddenly withdrawn. He stared at the grate, as if he already saw it leaping with flames. And then, although nothing moved there, I caught it too—the distant scent of wood smoke filtering through the masonry dust and the pop of wood as the fire (but there *was* no fire) crackled coldly.

"*She* loved the flames," Dad said in a voice that went nowhere. "Every one was a living thing to her—a brief, pure, beautiful life. Like her own." The last words racked a shudder out of him. The fire that was not there fizzed, rattled with sappy moisture, and subsided.

"Who?" I asked softly.

He turned, and smiled at me. I think he'd forgotten I was there. "Your mother, of course, love. Now, why don't you leave me to my work? There's still a lot to do."

He knelt by the fire and started to examine the inside of the grate. After a few moments he started whistling "My Way."

That did it—Frank Sinatra broke the spell. At once it was impossible to see anything there but Dad. The fear extinguished itself for lack of air. I'd been imagining things.

Still, there was something I had to make sure of.

Time was when everyone played "Greensleeves"; but recently our Electricity Board had graduated to the 1970s. Perhaps they'd got a new executive in charge of Muzak Operations. Anyway, it was "Hotel California" coming down the line as I hung on in the one phone booth on my paper route, watching the units on my phone charge card tick down to zero. Something mellow to make you think, "Hey, it's only money, maaaan." But it wasn't only money, it was the last five units on my phone card. And this was important.

"Hello? Hello, my name's Petra McCoy. Of 69 The Rise, Cooper's Bridge."

"Could you give me your account number, please?" chirped the voice at the other end.

I reeled off the number from our last bill. I knew where Dad kept them—it hadn't been hard to find.

There was a pause as she tapped the number into the computer. "You're two months in arrears," she said in a conversational way. "You realize you're due to be cut off on Friday?"

"We're already cut off!" I exclaimed.

"No, I don't think so," the voice explained. "Friday the seventh, it says here. Are you the account holder?"

I told her as well as I could about the storm and the tree.

But now it was impossible to get the voice off the subject of our unpaid bill. "We have flexible schemes to help customers who get into difficulties. If you'll just hold the line, I'll put you through—"

"No!" I shouted. I looked at the meter. Three units and counting. "I'm not calling about the bill."

"It is two months in arrears, you know."

"Yes, yes, I know that."

"Then what *are* you ringing about?"

I'd got her attention, but now she sounded suspicious, as if I'd been stringing her along all this time about our bill.

"I'm calling to find out if my father—that's Mr. Richard McCoy—has asked you to reconnect us. After the storm, I mean. When we got disconnected," I added.

"Well, I don't know, I'll have to see . . ."

The voice wandered off somewhere. In the distance, questions were being tossed backward and forward across an office the size of Wembley Stadium. There were shouted replies and laughter, too, which I tried to remember probably wasn't directed at me.

There were two units left on my card.

The voice returned. "Hello? No, there's been no request for reconnection. Have you given me the correct—"

"Thanks, 'bye!"

I slammed the phone down just before it spat out my card.

My godmother, Selina Button (who works in London and never visits), sends me a phone card for my birthday each year along with a note saying "Keep in touch!"—which I never do except for a quick call to say thank you (six units maximum). It must be the most exciting gift idea since underwear elastic. Still . . .

I lifted the receiver again and dialed.

"Yes?" Mel's voice, out of breath.

"Listen," I said rapidly. "About what you asked earlier. I've changed my mind. I do want to talk."

"What? Oh, right!" Mel couldn't hide the fact that she'd forgotten for a moment.

"Not on the phone, though. Tomorrow, early."

"Okay, come over. I'll be in the loft. Listen, are you all right?"

I bit my lip as a new thought occurred to me.

"And I need your help. There's something I've got to do."

Downstairs a door crashed shut.

Awake—I was awake, I realized—I snatched a look at my watch. The hands gleamed a guilty small-hours message: two-thirty, near as anything. Dad was moving about still, from room to room. I reached for the matches and lit the lamp.

He'd been going through my things. I couldn't help but see it. The room had rearranged itself in tiny ways no one but me would notice. The mess had been kicked back against the wall, leaving a path from the door to my bed where I could walk on real carpet. Having given up on sleep, I rolled out of bed and went to the dressing table. The scent bottle was still there. When I tilted it, the liquid inside was quickened by a thousand glints, moving together in a silver-backed shoal. My hand closed around the stopper and pulled, but it wouldn't budge now. Not for me.

The same thoughts rolled around again like unclaimed luggage. How Mr. Century had loved Eurydice Tremain. In some senile corner of his mind he'd thought I *was* Eurydice—he had tried to remake me in her image. And I had refused him, pushed him away. Pushed him where, though? Could all those years of guilt and grief just disappear? I doubted it.

Perhaps I hadn't pushed him very far at all . . .

I slammed the bottle down with a thud. Get a grip, get a grip! I'd led myself astray. I couldn't even be sure, if it came to it, that the Darkling had been more than a nightmare, boiled up from the leftovers of the last three days. It was gone now, I must remember that. Gone. Mr. Century was dead, as was Eurydice, and their story was a historical romance, just like *Plucked from the Burning.* If Dad was acting strangely, that was nothing unusual after all. Look at the car! And all those attempts to learn a foreign language, when he thought he might take the family to live abroad. It was always the same with him. So now he was thinking about living the good life, without electricity. He'd get over it as soon as he tired of lighting candles.

There was movement down in the kitchen and a faint, alluring smell of food. That was good. Late-night snacks were one of Dad's weaknesses. Mine, too—food always tastes better after you've brushed your teeth. I pulled my bathrobe on and went downstairs.

Dad was sitting at the kitchen table. Three candles were arranged around him and beside them a plastic tub of salt. The steam from a bowl of soup (tomato, by the smell) wafted into his face. He looked down through it as if he were staring over the lip of a volcano.

"Got the munchies?" I moved around him to the other side of the table.

He ignored me, except to sit up straight and start eating. He

ate the soup as Mum had always tried and failed to get me and
Jamie to do, with the spoon moving politely away from his body.
I wanted to remember if Dad had always eaten soup that way,
but couldn't. It's not the kind of thing you notice till you start
to look.

The fridge light didn't come on anymore. No wave of cold
air washed around my feet, just the smell of food turning the last
corner on the road to ruin. I had put the milk in a bowl of water
to keep it cool, but by now little flecks of yellow were forming
on the surface. Good enough for hot chocolate, anyway. I
slammed the door shut, harder than I'd meant, and braced
myself for the usual shower of fridge magnets. Nothing happened. All the bills, the special offers—and the Family
Contract, too—had disappeared.

"Hey, where's the Contract?"

The spoon paused halfway to Dad's mouth, and he looked at
me sharply. "It's been rescinded."

"*What?*" I wasn't too sure what rescinded meant, but it
didn't sound very pleasant.

"Circumstances have changed," he added as the spoon
resumed its journey. The words were shot at me like arrows. His
mouth was the thinnest of slits.

"What do you mean? What circumstances?"

He turned in his chair and said with a sudden, labored
patience: "I mean I've got a job, of course. I'm not going to have
time to be cooking you dinner every other day."

"Oh, I see!"

Any other time I'd have argued with him. After all, school's
a full-time job, too, isn't it? But I was so relieved to hear him talk

like that—like Dad, I mean, even if he was being unreason-
able—I didn't press the point. "You should go to bed," I said
instead. "You've had a long day." I didn't like to see him sitting
there alone.

"Ever heard of the pot and the kettle?" Now he was moving
the spoon back the other way, toward him. His back was no
longer ramrod straight, but arched over the food protectively as
usual.

"But you've been hard at it for hours. You must be fit to
drop."

Suddenly he did look tired. The candles showed up the lines
in his face, the bags under his eyes slung like hammocks. "It's
true," he admitted, "I don't know where the time went. One
minute I was doing those sketches for Graham, and the next I
knew the clock was striking midnight. I was still up to my knees
in broken bricks."

My hand froze over the cup. "You mean you really don't
remember?"

"Sorry?"

"This evening? You don't remember anything about it?"

It still took him a moment to understand. "I wasn't talking
literally, love," he said with a laugh.

"Well, no, of course—"

"I'm not quite senile yet!"

I made a fuss about pouring the milk into my mug. "Of
course not."

"So long as that's understood!" He spooned some more soup
from the bowl, smacking his lips. "You seem very edgy," he added.

"Do I?"

"Very, all day. Been sleeping all right?"

"Why do you ask?"

"Because"—he blew at his spoon, though the soup must have been cool enough by this time—"because of what happened last night. You got a fright, when the tree fell."

"I can't sleep at all, if you want to know. That's why I came down."

The kettle whistled for attention, and I took it off the flame. As I poured, the reflection of the room behind me grew and shrank along the curved sides of the kettle. The fridge door, white and naked without the magnets. The hooks over the sink. And there at the table, something in the shape of a man. A tilt of the kettle gave it a hugely bulbous head and shrank the rest to doll size. It was staring into my back. The eyes were hungry—animal. Not Dad's eyes. I was looking at the Darkling itself. I think it saw me, too, because at once the head dropped down, like a marionette string being cut. It started to eat again.

My hand began to shake, sloshing water over the stove top.

"Grip hard," said the Darkling, and now it didn't bother with Dad's voice. "You don't want to spill a single drop."

"No," I said, my voice trembling as much as my hand. "I'll be careful."

The Darkling's mouth flapped open, and a slow stream of spittle snaked toward the table. I slammed the kettle onto the stove top and spun around. The spoon was moving back to the bowl, slow as lava.

I ran for the door.

"Hey, where do you think you're going?" asked my dad, starting to stand. "Petra?"

I scrambled up the stairs to my room and locked the door. My whole body was shaking. "Oh God, oh God!" I sank to the floor and put my head into my arms. Dad did not follow me. He did not come upstairs. He was still down in the kitchen, eating soup. A spasm shot from my stomach to my heart and brain. Something inside me was dying.

I prayed he'd stay down there forever.

11

Personal Effects

IT WAS THE MORNING AFTER the first frost. In the woods above the Composers' Estate, the grass was still stiff with ice, but dew from the overhanging branches had begun to puncture it with cold, heavy drops. Gradually the grass yielded, as a slow scythe of light swept toward the trees. But in the deepest part of the wood, where the lane wound its way up toward Century Hall, even that thin blade of warmth could not penetrate.

I waded through the leaf drifts, kicking until my feet were sodden. A few paces behind, Mel was more cautious as she hopped from one stiff ridge of mud to another. A fisherman's sweater rose above her chin and drooped almost to her knees. The climb and the cold weather had made Mel pink, like a Christmas card carol singer, but no warmth rose in me to drive back the cold. I thought I must be white as snow.

"Slow down, it's not a race!" Mel called as I drew ahead again. I checked myself and allowed her to come level. No, it wasn't a race. I fidgeted with the strap of my shoulder bag, anxious to have done with it all the same.

"Don't you think you're getting things out of proportion?" she offered, trying to flush me out.

"No," I said. "If you'd seen him, you'd understand."

"I only wish I could!"

"It's like living with a stranger. One minute he seems normal, and the next . . . he's so *cold*. Like this morning. Normally he's half asleep first thing. It's all he can do to keep from spreading coffee on his toast. But today he was a robot, all so neat and clean and perfect. He even offered me the sugar, like I was the vicar come to visit. He never does that, never! I looked up once, and he was just staring at me over the paper, with this neat little smile stitched to his face. As if he'd got some nasty surprise lined up for me. Mel, I didn't recognize him."

"That's probably because he was in a suit. No, don't start— you said yourself he went a bit hyper when he got this job. It's spooked him, that's all. And it's spooked you, too. It doesn't mean it's got anything to do with your dream."

"It wasn't a dream."

"I'm sorry—I should have said 'vision'!" She raised her angelic face to heaven.

"All right. Why should I expect you to believe me? All I know is I'm going to see Mrs. Campbell." I hitched my shoulder bag higher. "You don't have to come."

"Of course I'll come! But you must admit, it's all a bit hard to take. A *ghost* is trying to take over your father?"

"I didn't say it was a ghost."

"What then?"

"A spirit, a soul—I don't know! Whatever's left of us after we die. The dregs."

"Sounds like a ghost to me. Honestly, why not admit you two had a row? That's what's at the bottom of it."

"You'll believe what you like, naturally."

"Me and my old man are at it all the time. You should have heard us the other day. Subject? The sin of riding into patients' houses on horseback. Fur and feathers flew, Petra! Mummy ran to the garden with her pruning shears and wasn't seen until tea time. Even my dear brother fled the house. But then it was kiss and make up, and now I'm Daddy's favorite darling girl again. The air is clear, the birds sing."

I pretended not to have heard. But then I found myself asking, "So that's why Lee was in town on Sunday?"

"You saw him, did you? He kept very quiet about that. What a sly one! Oh, Petra, it must be love. He's bought up every skin-care product in the Western world. The medicine cabinet's just oozing. He's obviously trying to clean up his act, and all for you."

"Why, what's he said?"

"As if he'd confide in his little sister! But he doesn't need to—he's an open book. The love light's in his eyes."

"I'm happy for him," I said ungraciously.

"You *are* in a mood this morning, aren't you? I'm only trying to spread some happiness . . ." Mel was not offended, however, and seemed determined to glitter. Perhaps it was her way of keeping nerves at arm's length.

A final corkscrew bend brought us out of the woods, and at the same time the lane gave way to gravel. Beech trees lined the approach to the Hall, and beyond them a pair of pillars marked the courtyard entrance. The Hall settled itself before us, arms extended, hunched like a sphinx.

"Are you sure you want to go through with this?" asked Mel.

"Chickening out?"

"I only mean, what will you say to her? 'Will you please call off your boss? He's haunting my dad.'"

"It's the truth, isn't it?" But the truth was I hadn't thought what I would say to Mrs. Campbell. When I had decided to come to the Hall, it had seemed the obvious thing to do. Mrs. Campbell was the only person who might know what was going on. Now, as I approached the porch, reached out for the iron bell pull, and heard our arrival announced to the deserted yard, I realized I had no plan of any kind. And now it was too late.

"No one's in," said Mel. "Come on, let's go back."

"No. I heard something."

I put my hand against the door. Unnervingly it yielded, then yawned open.

Mel made a theatrical *creeeak* at the back of her throat. "Anybody home?"

The hallway was empty. It was more than empty—it was stripped. The side table with its brass oil lamp, the pair of mirrors that sent the light cascading to infinity, all gone. My heel squeaked against the floorboards, scuffing a spray of dirt across the floor. The end of the hallway was in shadow. My hand brushed a wire, and I traced it down till I came up against the familiar shape of a telephone. As I lifted it, the receiver fell unattached to the floor.

"Mel, look here."

She glanced in from the doorway. "Must've got broken in the move. Someone was in a hurry to get out of here." She shivered dramatically, but it was only half an act. "Can't say I blame them. Come on, Petra, your housekeeper isn't around. Let's go."

"Not yet. I want to know what's happened." Mel was still hovering in the porch. "Well, are you coming in?"

She sighed. "I'm coming! Just what is it you want to find out?"

"Everything," I declared; then added lamely, "There must be some kind of clue."

"A clue, of course! What shall we look for first? A blood-stained hanky? Or are we going straight for the poison fountain pen? Jeepers!"

I pushed open the door at the end of the hall, the door to Mr. Century's room. I was trying not to think of ghosts, but when a fluttering white figure rose up and started through the air toward me, I stepped back into Mel with fright—then felt foolish as I saw the lace curtains billowing in the draft of the open window. This room, too, was empty: only Mr. Century's chair sat as it always had, within poker's reach of the fire. Without its many blankets, it was nothing much to look at. Just a ruinous piece of junk, not worth stealing. A yellow stain ran the length of its pale cushions. Ashes from the fireplace were blown everywhere in a gloomy confetti.

Mel backed out of the room uneasily. I lingered, hoping the empty space would yield some kind of secret. I knew Mel was right of course—it was stupid to look for clues. Life wasn't an Agatha Christie novel. But after getting up the nerve to come in the first place I felt cheated . . .

"Petra! In here!"

I ran from the room and across the hall. Mel's call had come from an alcove on the far side of the corridor, where a pair of heavy doors had been unbolted and flung open. Mel was standing in the middle of a long, narrow room.

"Welcome to Eldorado!"

After the hallway, the color here was startling. Every wall was covered with bright patterns of leaves and fruit, gilded oriental scenes, scrolls with gaudy mottos. Here and there, groups of stuffed animals and birds stood facing each other: rat and dog and eagle were gathered together in unlikely conversations. A lattice of metal vines curled out to twine itself about the nearest pillar.

"Just look at this!" Mel pointed to one of the painted scrolls. The messages ran all around us.

Wherein have I sinned?

What duty have I neglected?

Practice justice in words and deeds!

And above our heads, in gold:

Reverence thy oath!

"It's like my old Sunday school," said Mel, but this time she didn't seem to think it was funny. She was staring, like me.

The floor tiles were laid out in geometrical patterns. A mosaic of angles spiraled in toward a wide disc of burnished copper. When we moved nearer, the metal shone softly back. Another room was captured in its reflection, caged by the beams from a skylight above our heads. Looking up, I saw the room had a second level, a long balcony with a metal rail. The walls there were lined with shelves—remains of a library, perhaps. Nearby ran two long rows of ill-assorted book spines: some thick and ancient, others seemingly new.

"Here's a blast from the past," called Mel. She was holding a huge, fragile book, with a ribbed spine dangling by a single piece of twine. It was laid open at the first page, where the word OPERA was carved like a stone inscription. Opposite stood an engraving of a man in a long wig, half High Court judge, half guitar legend. His body was partly turned away, as if he couldn't spare the artist much more of his time, but the sardonic smile was untroubled and instantly familiar. "William Century F.R.S." was written in curly letters underneath.

"It's a collection of his books, all bound together," said Mel, leafing though it. "See, the pages aren't even the same size, and—look, here's your bloodstain!" Where the book had fallen open the paper was discolored by a large brown blot. It could have been anything. It could have been blood. "'The Blunting of Atropos' Shears or The Three Sisters Confuted.' Oh, Petra, listen to this! 'The Occult Discipline made Plain, whereby the Adept may outlive his mortal Body at the Day of Dissolution.' Sounds handy."

"Fascinating," I muttered. As Mel relaxed, I seemed to be growing more nervous. The idea of laughing at William Century made me uneasy.

"There's plenty more where that came from. 'Salmacis' Prayer Granted: Showing the Ceremony for the Conjunction of True-loving Souls, through Oaths sealed in Fire and Sacrifice, Englished'—Englished, I like that—'from the Book of Ibn Alhaz—'"

Somebody sneezed.

I looked up, just in time to see a door opening at the far end of the gallery. Instinctively, I grabbed Mel and dragged her to the side of the room, underneath the balcony. It suddenly occurred to me that we had no right to be exploring Century Hall.

"Has he any objection?"

It was a man's voice—gruff, offhand. The wrong voice for a room like this. I couldn't take my eyes from the floor, where William Century's book lay as it had fallen. His face stared mockingly at us from the frontispiece. I hoped whoever was on the balcony above our heads would be too busy to notice.

"On the contrary," replied another man. This voice was plum colored. Whoever owned it must be tall and wearing a tailored suit. "He was anxious to wrap matters up as soon as possible. Frankly, I think he needs the capital quite promptly."

"A convenient windfall, then. Good job he's out of the country, or people might get the wrong idea!"

A third voice laughed, a laugh that cut through the air like a saw.

"My client's got nothing to fear there," said the plummy voice. "He was quite unaware of Mr. Century's existence, let alone his own position. It seems there was some kind of family rift a generation back. Toby's worked very hard to find him. Even I've had to practice my French on some country solicitors."

"So long as you can get his agreement. I'm sure I can guide it through the committee. Which just leaves your end, Graham. You've been a bit quiet. You're not losing your enthusiasm, are you?"

"I hadn't had a chance to look around inside before, that's all. The place is sound enough, I can see that. Those weak beams would be going anyway. But I hadn't expected such a mess."

"Superficial, mostly. The old man didn't go overboard on home decoration."

"I suppose not." Graham sneezed again. "Come on, let's get back into the fresh air! The dust in here disagrees with me."

Their footsteps passed overhead. Another door opened, and there was a bit of joking as they all tried to hold it for each other. Then silence.

Mel swung away from me and gasped. I think she'd been holding her breath the whole time. "This thing's bigger than both of us," she said weakly. "I suggest a vacation."

"Suits me," I answered. I felt exhausted. We waited five cautious minutes, then left the library, Mel leading. In the porch she stopped and drew me into cover.

"I thought sheepskin jackets went out with the ark!" she hissed.

"What?"

"That man who was just here—he dresses like a football manager."

"Haven't they gone?"

"They're nattering out there in the yard. Sheepskin is clapping one of the others in the back. I don't think he liked that very much—I guess he must be the toffee-nosed one. And now he's shaking hands with Sneezy—"

"Graham Cooke," I corrected automatically.

"You know him?"

"He's my dad's boss," I admitted.

"Well, no wonder you don't want him to see you here! Anyway, you can come out, they're walking off together—three jolly swagmen. Left the front door open, too. Do they live in a barn?"

I stepped past her into the shade of the porch. I didn't feel able to cope with Mel just now or her way of skating across the surface of situations. I couldn't cope with any of it: Mrs. Campbell's disappearance, the library—and especially not Graham Cooke. On the far side of the courtyard, three men were walking, hideously distinct in the bright sunshine. Graham strolled a little apart from the others. As they reached the gates, he let his companions go on ahead, then turned to look back. Instinctively I slid behind the pillars into deeper shadow, though I knew he could not see me. I guessed what was in his thoughts. That sense of being watched, of squaring up against a living thing—I had experienced it myself, every time I came to Century Hall. Then he lifted his hat and tipped it, very polite. Smiling, and with a shake of the shoulders as if he was accusing himself of superstition, he hurried down the drive to join his friends.

12
Billy Goat Gruff

THAT EVENING Babushka brought Jamie home. I saw them from my bedroom window as her car drew up, a long station wagon with space in the back for a couple of wolfhounds. She hopped out and went to open Jamie's door. The peak of Jamie's baseball cap emerged, followed by the rest of him, looking small and blurry-faced. Babushka put her arm around his shoulder and guided him up the path.

I opened the door just as she reached for the bell.

"The hero returns!" announced Babushka as she ushered Jamie into the hall. "The hunter's home from the hill! Come on, let's not stand in the draft." She knew how to turn on a bustling air, and before I could say hello, she was organizing us in the direction of the kitchen.

"How are you feeling, James?" I asked with a sideways grin. Jamie might be a nuisance, but I'd missed him—more than I'd ever admit to his face. With Jamie in the house, everything would be down to earth and ordinary again. There was no way specters could take any liberties with him around—they'd be too embarrassed.

He smiled the kind of saintly smile he hadn't quite managed

when I visited before. "Okay," he replied simply. "Have you been feeding Giggs?"

Giggs was Jamie's gecko, who lived upstairs in an old aquarium with a pile of rocks and sand. "Giggs is in the pink. Or whatever color lizards are meant to be. What about you? Do you fancy a jaffa cake?"

"I'm going to see Dad," said Jamie, dropping his coat over a chair. "Is he in the workshop?"

"Yes, but hang on, Jamie, he won't want—"

Babushka took me by the shoulder. "Let him go, he's been dying to see his father." Then more quietly: "You know he hasn't visited?"

I hesitated, uncertain how much to say. "He *is* very busy. The new job—he may not have time . . ."

"To say hello to his own son?" Babushka scoffed. "Honestly, Petra, you do get some strange ideas." She sat on one of the white kitchen chairs, without taking off her overcoat. "Apart from anything else, he was the one who asked me to bring Jamie home tonight."

"He was?"

"If it had been up to me, I'd have kept him for a day or two yet. His throat's still very tender. Of course, he's dying to see the fireworks tomorrow, but that's out of the question."

"Did Dad sound—all right, on the phone?"

Again Babushka smiled. "Why on earth shouldn't he?"

"He's been in a mood—"

"It was a terrible line, now you mention it," Babushka said. "Something to do with this electrical trouble you've been having, I should think. *There's* another good reason for James staying on with me. A house without proper heat isn't the place for a convalescent."

That was true enough, but I thought she was a bit sorry to be losing her patient, too. Dad had been right about Babushka being a closet knitter at heart. "Do you want to stay to supper?" I asked, glad at the prospect of her company.

"I'd better be getting back, thanks, love. I've got to throw a six-foot transplant surgeon into Lisa Oakstock's path."

It took me a moment to realize she was talking about the heroine of her latest book. Babushka often spoke of her characters as if they were flesh-and-blood people. It could make conversations quite confusing. I tried to sound more interested than I felt. "Are they in love yet?"

"They've been in love from the moment they met," Babushka confided. "But they're both too proud and headstrong to admit it. Besides, he works all hours, and she has her own life to lead as a successful interior designer."

"It doesn't sound very romantic, Gran," I said, keeping my eyes on the door to the workshop.

"Oh, it will be by the time I've finished. I'm arranging a medical emergency at the Ideal Home Exhibition. That should bring them to their senses."

I couldn't tell whether she was joking. But the fate of her latest lovers didn't concern me either way—I knew *they'd* be all right in the end. I was listening for Dad and Jamie. That was why Babushka was still here, too, of course, instead of tearing back to her word processor. After she'd cosseted his son for three days, the least Dad could do was to come out and say hello. But Babushka hadn't seen Dad during those three days. She hadn't seen the way he could change, in the time it took to turn the page of a book, from his own chaotic self to silence and chilly anger.

Jamie was taking an awfully long time.

Someone knocked at the front door. I'd forgotten that knock, but as soon as I heard it, I knew it was Graham Cooke. Babushka went to let him in.

He looked surprised to see her. "Hello, you're Richard's mother, aren't you? I don't suppose you remember me?"

"I remember you very well, Mr. Cooke," Babushka corrected him. She always resented any suggestion she was less than razor sharp. But then she had reasons to resent Graham Cooke anyway. "You want to speak to Richard?"

"Is he about?" asked Graham, stepping into the hall. "It's all right, I'll find my own way."

Just then the door to Dad's workshop flew open, and Jamie ran out. I don't think he even saw the three of us as he made for the stairs. He had his hand in front of his face to cover the fact he was crying.

Dad was close behind him. I was nearest the workshop door, so I spotted him before the others—and to tell the truth, I'm glad Babushka never saw him in that state. His face was deathly pale, and his eyes were black—moist black, like pools of oil. He grabbed hold of the door and held on for dear life. He shook it back and forth, he was trembling so much. Something brutal was tearing at him from the inside. Then he saw Graham and snap!—it was as if someone had turned on a tap to let the color run back into his face. He stood up straight and even managed a smile as he stepped forward with his hand outstretched.

"Graham! This is an unexpected pleasure. Hello, Ma." He gave Babushka a peck on the cheek—or bestowed it rather. "Thanks for bringing back the prodigal. We've missed him in a funny sort of way, haven't we, Petra?" He grinned at me, as if we were all in on some great family joke.

Upstairs, Jamie's door slammed shut.

Babushka didn't know what to say. "What on earth's happened?" was the best she could do.

"Oh, we've been sorting out a few ground rules," said Dad. "Now, Graham, what brings you here?"

"What did you say to him?" Babushka stood between Dad and Graham, one hundred and fifty pounds of immovable overcoat. "He's been good as gold the last few days, and within five minutes of coming home he's in tears."

"I seem to have stumbled into a family reunion," commented Graham Cooke, with his usual lack of embarrassment. "Perhaps I should call back another time."

"Don't be daft—you just go into the living room and make yourself at home. Turn on the gas heater. Or would you like something to warm you from the inside out?"

"Thanks, I know where it is. Scotch and water for you?"

Graham left the hall but didn't shut the door behind him. Babushka had to reach across and pull it—almost, but not quite, hard enough to count as a slam.

"Now, what's going on?" she demanded.

"Nothing's going on," said Dad. "Don't make a fuss."

"I am *not* making a fuss! In case you hadn't noticed, James is still ill. It's looking after he needs, not a dressing-down from his father, whatever he said!"

Dad gave a snort of contempt. "I think that's between me and him, don't you?"

"I'm his grandmother!"

"Of course you are. It's a grandmother's right to spoil her grandchildren. But when they get back home, that's when the spoiling has to stop." He smiled, the spiteful little smile I'd never seen before two nights ago. "I don't recall your being so indulgent when I was Jamie's age."

"He's ill, Richard!" Babushka didn't know how to handle Dad like this. There was nothing to grab hold of in this sudden smooth front—nothing like Dad at all.

"Jamie's on the mend. A lesson in manners won't do him any harm."

"Oh, this is nonsense!" Babushka turned away in disgust and made toward the door. At the last moment, she looked back again. "What did he say that was so unforgivable anyway?"

"He didn't need to say anything to spoil three hours' good work. All he had to do was barge into my workshop when I was in the middle of some very *delicate* detail and throw himself around my neck like a young baboon."

"Well, he was pleased to see you! The way you talk, anyone would think it was brain surgery you were doing in there."

"It's my job I'm doing in there," declared Dad, very steadily.

"And of course that's the most important thing in the world!"

Dad smiled the same icy smile. "Of course."

"You're being ridiculous! I'll talk to you when you're capable of a reasonable discussion."

"As you wish."

"Right! Good night, Petra."

I followed her down the path. She was stomping back to the car, her head down as if she was about to ram it.

"Gran! Wait a minute!"

She heaved her shoulders and let out a two-lung sigh. "I'm sorry, Petra. I thought if I stayed in there another minute I'd say something I'd regret."

"Don't be angry," I found myself saying. "The job and everything—it's been more of a strain than he's letting on. He'll be okay, you'll see."

I don't know why I was covering up for Dad. I suppose I didn't want to be forced into explanations Babushka would never believe. I didn't want to believe them either. There was still part of me that hoped I'd got everything out of proportion, the way Mel had said.

"I ought to come back in," she said, suddenly undecided. "It doesn't seem right leaving you alone with him like this . . ."

"I'll be fine, Gran. You can't let Lisa Oakstock down. This will be forgotten in the morning."

"But I'm worried about Jamie. He's still not well—you should have heard him coughing last night."

"I'll look after Jamie, Gran. You know I will."

Babushka's shoulders sagged, and I knew she'd let herself be convinced. "Well, I'm only a phone call away. Remember that."

"I told you—in half an hour it'll be forgotten. You know Dad's moods."

A minute later the car was pulling into The Rise, with Babushka's hand fluttering at the window like a trapped moth. I watched till it reached the turn in the road, then went back in.

"Half an hour and it'll be forgotten," I repeated, hoping that rep-
etition might make the prediction true. But whatever truth it
had wore out with the retelling, and by the time I reached the
hallway, I knew it had been a lie.

Jamie didn't answer my knock. I took that as a *Yes*. He lay on
the bed with his clothes still on, just the top blanket pulled up
over him. Two candles burned on the windowsill. Giggs was
invisible as usual, a pair of bug eyes set in stone at the center of
his glass-framed universe.

"What do you want?"

"I brought you some hot chocolate. There's beans on toast,
too, if you like."

"I'm not hungry."

"Fair enough."

But he hiked himself up against the wall and took the mug
from me. I sat on the edge of the bed, unsure where to go from
here. How do you tell your little brother his dad's being *haunted*?
You don't, of course. Whatever had gone on between him and
Dad, Jamie had already seen enough to give him the jitters. I just
needed an ally, someone with a foothold in the ordinary world,
who could tell me for sure when things were normal and when
they weren't.

"I feel I should be reading you a bedtime story. I used to,
remember?"

Jamie paused, thinking of some smart answer to throw back
in my face. But he got the better of habit for once. "Course I do.
I used to love that. You couldn't do my favorite though."

"'Billy Goat Gruff'? 'I'm a troll, fol-de-rol!' I was brilliant!"

"You couldn't do the voice properly. Not like Mum."

Slurp from the mug. This child is a slob in the making. But you can't choose your family, can you?

Jamie has the look of Mum, sometimes. His hair is the same fleece of sooty blond. His eyes have the same green flecks—and that way of narrowing when he laughs, as if he saw something hilarious on the far horizon.

"Do you think about her a lot?" I asked. Jamie almost never mentioned her.

He considered this a long time, as though I'd asked some trick question in four-dimensional calculus. "I don't *think* about her. I *dream* about her sometimes."

"What do you dream?"

"How should I know? They're dreams, aren't they?" Slurp. "I think she's telling me off, mostly."

"Well, at least that's realistic!"

It was the wrong thing to say. "Just shut up about it. I'm going to sleep." He clapped the mug down and turned to the wall. He was breathing in tight, short bursts. I hadn't realized how close to tears he'd been, all this time. Great work, Petra. Clutching my life membership of the Big Mouth Club, I got up and blew the candles out.

Graham and Dad were settled in for an all-nighter. I could tell that from the way Graham's voice sounded as it came up the stairs, just a bit too loud for the words he was saying, and a bit too drunk to care. He seemed to be talking about Sarah Thrale.

"I know what you're going to say, Dick. But I was getting tired of her myself. She didn't know *what* she wanted. I was only trying to teach her to relax a bit . . ."

"Perhaps, perhaps."

Teeth, toilet, face and hands. It felt odd to be going through the routine by candlelight, just as if there was nothing unusual about it. My water glass was missing—I'd have to fetch another from the kitchen. A long groping walk down the stairs. Dad and Graham were quieter now, discussing business. I thought of Graham scornfully. If he was so clever, how could he fail to notice what was so obvious to me—that my father had *changed*? I had to admit, though, that Dad was doing a good imitation of himself, in half-cut mode. You'd have to listen very carefully to hear the Darkling's voice woven into his. You'd have to be like me and *know*. I fetched the glass. When I got back to the foot of the stairs, Graham was still talking.

"Infill, that's the point. You've got to think in the long term, Dick. Once there's an access road linking up with the Composers' Estate, we'll have twenty acres of prime land encircled, doing nothing very much in particular." There was a pause as Graham took a sip from his glass. "At which point—well, the pressures of an expanding urban population, you understand, may turn out to justify—"

"More musical streets?" Dad laughed. "They'll be running out of composers."

"Jim's into the French Impressionists these days, as a matter of fact. Or Dutch Masters. They're the latest thing—he's done a survey."

"Idiot!"

"That's all years down the line, anyway. But if it works out, well, someone's got to build those houses. More to the point, someone's got to design them."

"And you can trust Jim to aim the job the right way?"

"We've worked together before—why spoil a good thing? Talking of which, a bit less water in the next one if you don't mind."

I went to bed. I'd heard a hundred surefire schemes hatched over whiskey and water in that room. So this one involved Century Hall and some way to make money out of it—so what? Flats, or a hotel: I could picture the sort of thing. I'd seen enough flash prospectuses from Dad's years at Barlow's. Another time I might have cared, not now. Only I remember thinking, as I fell asleep, that Graham and his friends must have had it all planned out for months, to get so quickly off the mark. They must have been waiting for that death up at the Hall, perhaps a bit impatiently. I slept; and when I dreamed, I seemed to see Graham in Mr. Century's place beside the fire. His body was draped around with blankets, and shadows played upon his sleeping face. And the hearth shot sparks and ashes through the room, and waves of heat rolled out to batter him; until his face crumpled like a paper mask, and only the crucible of fire was left.

13

Remember, Remember

DAD **SPENT ANOTHER DAY** locked in his workshop—literally locked. I heard the key turn whenever he went
back after his occasional dashes into the kitchen for food or
drink. Even these excursions appeared too much like sociability
for him. He became an unseen, unspoken-of presence in the
house.

As for Jamie, he drifted through his transformed home as if
he hardly recognized the place. In the afternoon a couple of his
friends called round—Mig and Tony—and for a while they made
a show of doing holiday things: football in the garden, explo-
rations of the junk Dad had left in the sitting room. The idea of a
wood-burning hearth seemed to have been abandoned halfway,
leaving an inviting pile of rubble for investigation by nine-year-
olds. The fireplace became an ancient tomb, with Jamie and Tony
as archaeologists and Mig as the Cursed Thing that shambled
through its ruins. But Jamie had forgotten how to play. When Mig
began to roar, I caught Jamie glancing nervously toward the
workshop door, afraid Dad might burst out like a pantomime
demon spitting smoke. Tony and Mig left soon afterward.

I had to leave, too, to do my paper route for Mr. Harlow. He was in a rotten mood and seemed disappointed I wasn't late enough to give him the pleasure of telling me off. By way of making up for it, he added a new street to my route: "Now that Century Hall's order has lapsed." I worked my way through the Composers' Estate, slotting news into people's houses. It was while I was on my way back that the explosions started. First a streak of red stars above the nearby roofs—then two more, in green and gold. For a weird moment I thought they were coming from Century Hall. Then I remembered that this was Fireworks Night.

You have to understand about Fireworks Night in Cooper's Bridge. It used to be a small affair, with a few doddery men from the Rotarians letting off rockets, and a sports jacket standing in for Guy Fawkes. Then came Ted Deakin. Ted was a man with Hollywood ideas. The displays became larger and more spectacular. Soon a disc jockey arrived, fast-food vans, a small fun fair. It became an event in the Cooper's Bridge calendar, a calendar with very few events to compete. Everyone knew Ted. Dad knew him from the pub, and somehow he'd ended up as one of his annual assistants, rushing around behind ropes under Ted's impeccable baton.

Apparently Ted Deakin would be one helper short this year. Back home, the kitchen was dark. The faintest glimmer of light ringed the door to Dad's workshop, but he didn't answer when I called.

"Come on, Dad! Your country needs you!"

I knocked with the corner of my bike light.

"Gunpowder, treason, and plot! How can you resist?"

I was almost back in the hall when I heard the key turn. Dad was standing in the doorway, in his shirtsleeves. He looked as if he hadn't washed or slept for days. His clothes were rumpled, and his hair was a series of greasy furrows where he'd been running his fingers back. He hung there like a picture, his eyes fixed on me in a strange appeal.

"Are you coming?" I asked. I was determined to sound as normal as possible, but even to my own ears the brittle cheeriness rang false.

"Why do you do it?" he asked. He spoke so quietly that I could hardly make out the words.

"I'm sorry?"

"Why do you continue to torment me?"

"I only asked if you wanted to—"

"I know what you asked!" he bellowed. His voice shook me like a thunderclap. I wanted to run, but dared not turn my back on him. "You know the sight of you is a torture to me!" He lurched forward and leaned heavily on the table, as if he really were being racked out inch by inch. "Yet you act as if you didn't realize. To me you're just the shadow of what I might have had!"

"Dad!"

"Don't call me that!"

He was still staring at the tablecloth. He couldn't bring himself to look at me. "I'm no good without her, don't you see?"

I hesitated. Was he talking about Mum? "She's dead, Dad. Dead and buried. You have to let her go."

"Let her go?" He looked aghast. "You don't know what you're saying. Alone into the dark, forever? Oh, you're cruel!"

Mum, or Eurydice? Did he even know the difference anymore?

He leaned forward, horribly confiding. "I brought her home,
you see. No one suspected. The soil was still fresh, I muffled the
wheels."

His eyes were blank and glistening. The voice stretched
tight. I could not see Dad at all.

"You—you moved the body?"

"If I could see her face again! This time love would bind us
forever . . ." His expression changed, and he stood up straight.
"But you didn't want her to live, did you? You had to smother
her, before she'd even had a chance to breathe!"

"Not me, Dad!" I cried, backing away. His features blurred
as they darkened into anger. "I'm here to help you!"

"I don't need your help!" He turned on me. "I only want you
to get out of here! Just get out, now!"

Jamie was already waiting as I scrambled to the top of the
stairs. I don't know how much he'd heard. Too much.

"Grab your coat, Jamie. It's time we got to the Common."

"What's going on?" He backed away as if he was afraid I'd
punch him.

"The big fireworks display, of course. Move, or we'll miss
the start."

"Why was Dad shouting? Is he coming, too?"

"I expect he'll come later," I snapped. I saw more questions
and prevented them the only way I knew how, with a fiver from
my bag. He must have felt my hand shake as I gave it to him. "A
present from Gran. For video games, or cotton candy, whatever."

"But Gran doesn't want me to go tonight," he objected,

pocketing the money. "She said I wasn't well enough."

"You can give it back if you're going to argue."

"All right, I'm coming!" He dashed into his room to grab his coat from the floor.

We descended the stairs in silence. Dad was back in his workshop. I let myself out, and Jamie gently pulled the door to. We didn't need to speak to share the awful secret—that we were making our escape.

As we left The Rise, we joined a stream of walkers, all descending through the smoky air to the center of Cooper's Bridge. At intervals we'd hear the crack of fireworks from somebody's back garden or see a single rocket flare into the low clouds. Children ran back and forth along the pavement, waving luminous whips of green plastic or pestering their parents for sparklers. A mist gathered around our feet.

Soon the babble of children was drowned by the seventies disco coming from a caravan beside the Common. Nearby stood the fast-food vans and fairground stalls. Jamie disappeared instantly into the crowd—I lost sight of his cap threading its way toward the toffee apples. Well, he'd come to no harm there, apart from the usual fillings. I allowed myself to catch my breath. At the far end of the Common, the ground was roped off for the fireworks display. In another corner was the bonfire itself. It had been growing steadily over the last two weeks, a monument of packing cases and kindling, with an old armchair balanced at the top. The figure of the Guy was scarcely visible.

A laser kicked in, slicing a sharp green light through the mist. Smoke was pouring onto the Common all the time. It streamed from every fast-food van, poured from the pans and onion grills. The disco gave way to piped music, pumped from a spider-shaped ride that sent children flitting like bats through the fanning laser. I moved toward it and tried my luck at the shooting gallery. A series of battered metal tanks flashed up before me. I shot and won a blue rabbit I'd have paid good money not to own—but now, as usual, some scruple disabled me from dropping it in the nearest bin, so I stuffed it into my jacket pocket. I wandered like this for twenty minutes, letting money dribble away in little packets of artificial fun. It was easier, somehow, than forcing my mind back to Dad.

"Petra! Over here!" Someone had spotted me through the smoke. It was Vicky Davies from school. She was only yards away, but to reach her I had to struggle through a flash flood of enthusiasts for the spider ride. Vicky was short and plump, always jumping up to see what was going on beyond the surrounding heads. We were friends, but I knew she'd only called me over to show off her latest acquisition—a leather-clad senior called Tariq who was all set to go to the University. Tariq's presence at Vicky's side had raised her in the opinion of everyone whose opinion mattered.

They were standing at one of the old-fashioned stalls—the kind where you have to hit three playing cards with three darts to win a scoop of jelly beans. Tariq had one dart left.

"Go for the hearts!" urged Vicky romantically. "Tariq plays for the youth club," she added, turning to me. "He's really good, aren't you, Tar?"

"It's a bit different," Tariq said grimly. "These things are blunt as hell." He was drawing back his arm when Vicky squealed, "The ace, the ace!"

The dart landed in the ace of hearts, tipped slowly down, and fell to the table below.

"Vicky! Why'd you shout like that? You put me off."

"Never mind, you were very close," said Vicky, blandly. "Want a go, Petra?"

"Sure." It seemed one way to keep the peace. I pushed the money toward a man with a change bag strapped about his waist, received some darts in return, and threw one.

"Careful, Petra!" exclaimed Vicky. "You'll have someone's eye out!"

"At least she hit a card," said Tariq.

"Beginner's luck," I said. But I was more careful with the next dart. I hit the card I was after, one of the middle clubs. On the third, though, a surge in the crowd knocked my hand sideways.

"Oh, tough luck!" cried Vicky. The dart had missed the board altogether and dropped into the grass.

I snorted. "I was right the first time. Beginner's luck."

"Here, let me." A figure standing behind me leaned over and threw an object over my head. A dart was now sticking out from the six of spades.

"Hoy! We have a winner here!"

I turned to see Lee Gaspard. How long had *he* been standing there? The stall owner, who had wandered away to serve some other customers, came slowly back. He checked the darts, scooped some jelly beans into a paper bag, and handed them over—all without speaking.

"There you are," said Lee at my elbow. "Congratulations." He placed his unused darts on the edge of the stall and pulled me into the crowd.

I was annoyed at being hijacked like that. "I suppose you're waiting for me to thank you?"

"I don't think it would do you any harm. Or are you still worried about cheating?"

"I thought it was really neat," said Vicky in admiration. "He didn't see a thing."

"They're going to light the bonfire in a minute," said Tariq. "Come on, Vick, let's get a good position."

"These are yours." I thrust the bag of jelly beans toward Lee. "No thanks," he said with a grimace. "Bad for the complexion."

In the glow of the laser and the fun fair stalls, Lee's face shone down at me. Perhaps the lighting helped, but I thought Mel was right—Lee showed a definite improvement. He might even have been called good looking, if he'd had a floppy cravat and a jutting chin. If he'd just rescued me from a burning mansion he might even have been called handsome. But he had only won me a bag of jelly beans, and that wasn't enough.

I took the toy rabbit from my jacket. "Then you must have this instead—or how can I ever thank you?"

He cradled the thing in his hand. "I'll carry it always. And here, in return"—he delved into his own pocket and retrieved one of the luminous strips being sold around the Common— "please wear this and think of me."

"I couldn't. It must have set you back at least the price of a hot dog."

"What's money compared with friendship?" He took my hand gently—his own was warm from the fleece of his pocket— and clipped the strip around my wrist. For the first time I actually saw his eyes. They were soft, a deep and marbled gray.

"Thank you," I said quietly. The sound of the spider ride seemed to subside for a moment, as if someone had gently closed a door behind us. In the reflection of his eyes, I saw the first flames of the bonfire flicker near the churchyard. Then they were blotted out, and his expression changed.

A man barged violently forward and sent Lee sprawling into the mud. An ugly voice snarled beside me: "Watch where you're putting your hands!" The man walked up to Lee, one foot poised as if he was about to kick him; then he swerved aside abruptly and paced toward the bonfire. It only took a couple of seconds.

Lee got to his feet slowly. He wasn't hurt. His jacket had a few dark patches where he'd landed in the mud, but it was meant to be khaki anyway. He watched the man walk, then break into a run as he approached the crowds near the fire. "Who *was* that? Do you know that guy?"

I took in the man's long-paced stride, the set of his shoulders. I drew a deep breath. "No, I don't know him."

"I think he knew you."

"Well, you're wrong."

Lee had the good sense not to press the point. We didn't follow Dad down to the bonfire but drew nearer the church, where the road was lined with cars. I was looking for Jamie, but it was impossible to pick anyone out of the milling darkness. No doubt he was already roasting in the hot breath of the fire. Right up against the guide ropes if I knew him.

"We must stop meeting like this," I said, thinking how surprising it was. How surprising that I should find myself with Lee after all.

"Where would you like us to meet?" he replied promptly.

"Oh, somewhere in a forest glade, maybe. In distant Zelmar."

"Suits me."

"Huh. Except you never leave your room, do you?"

"I'm here, aren't I?" he asked, feigning surprise. "What about the other day?"

"Exceptions prove the rule," I persisted. "Everyone knows your brain's made of silicon. You have to plug it into the electric current eight hours a night."

He gave a hollow laugh. "I can see someone's been spreading rumors about me."

"You mean they exaggerated?"

He paused. "I'm quite hurt."

"Then prove me wrong."

"Please do not cross the barriers. They are there for your protection."

We looked toward the crowd near the fire. It seemed to be rippling. Some disturbance had sent a shock wave through it.

"What's going on?" said Lee, taking me by the hand and running toward the crowd. I don't know how, but he sensed the panic that had seized me. I stumbled after, as the crowd bubbled forward, then parted to let two men in dark uniforms rush to the fire. People at the back were craning to see, and there was a lot of pointing that had nothing to do with the scheduled entertainment. We found ourselves alongside Ted Deakin. He was wearing a luminous orange jerkin and carried a flashlight that he used like a ray gun to cut a path through the bodies.

"What's going on?"

"They're throwing water!"

"Lunatic!"

"Let go then!"

"There you are!"

That was Mel. She was running toward us, away from the ropes. She spread her arms out to block our path. "You don't want to go through there. Come on."

"What's happening?"

"I'll tell you. Now, *come!*"

She pushed us back through the crowd. Even now I saw the look of quick understanding with which she took in me and Lee. But that was for another time.

"It's your father," she said.

"Is he all right? The ambulance men, they were—"

"He's fine," she interrupted. "He never got near the flames."

"Are you sure this was Petra's father?" asked Lee, defensively. "This isn't one of your bad jokes?"

Mel gave him a withering look. "Petra's sure, aren't you, Petra?"

I nodded. I was sure all right. "What happened?"

"He ducked under the ropes when the stewards had just lit the fire. They didn't seem too bothered at first. Some of them recognized him—guess they thought he'd come to help. Then he started shouting his head off. I couldn't hear all the words, but he was trying to make out there was someone trapped on top of the bonfire. No one else could see anything up there except that stupid Guy. When he realized he wasn't getting anywhere, he just laid out one of the stewards—wham! A good solid right to the jaw! Then he started climbing over the packing cases. It took three of them to pull him down, and even then he was still swinging."

"Where is he? I've got to find him." I tried to push past Mel, but she held me back.

"They took him out to the road. He's gone. You'll never get through to him that way."

I hesitated, long enough for another thought to whack me from behind. "Jamie! He must have seen everything."

"Jamie's here?"

Almost at once I saw Jamie's baseball cap and lime green coat weaving through the crowd fifty yards away. I shook myself free of Lee and Mel and pushed through the hustle of bodies.

"Jamie!"

The cap paused momentarily, but then moved on, skirting the ropes to the far side of the fire. I dived under the rope, trying to cut him off.

Someone pulled me back roughly by the arm.

"No you don't. We've had enough of that for one night." A light was flashing in my face. "Back under the rope—come on, I haven't got time to waste."

"Mr. Deakin? Mr. Deakin?"

He lowered the light, and I recognized Ted Deakin's trowel-shaped face through the red-and-blue flashes dancing in my eyes. "Did someone send you?"

"My dad—where is he?"

The flashlight twitched back up to my face. He didn't know me. "I'm Petra McCoy. My father—"

"Oh, I see." He was taken by surprise. "Your father's fine—cuts and bruises, that's all. But they're taking him to Bournemouth General for safety's sake. You'd better come with me." He swung the light around and led me off to the Stewards'

Caravan. It's amazing what an orange jerkin can do. People made way for him as if he were an oncoming train. At the top of the trailer steps stood Jamie. He was staring out toward the bonfire. The last of the flames were hissing themselves into steam.

"Jamie?" I stood in front of him, but he didn't move. He didn't take his eyes away from the fire.

"I'm going to phone Gran—she'll fetch us."

He nodded slightly. Jamie was in there somewhere. But he was still staring into space when the fireworks began five minutes later. And he was still staring when Babushka's car jerked to a halt in the road beside the Common.

14

The Resurrection Man

THE PHONE WAS RINGING in Babushka's living room. She glanced at me, but I shook my head. I did not want to take the call.

Jamie was too busy even to notice. Just now he was picking the chocolate chips out of Babushka's cookies, to keep them in a neat pile at the side of his plate for later. He seemed to have recovered from the night before—I even found myself wondering how much he remembered. Babushka drew in a breath and rose from the table. She paused at the kitchen door to move the calendar on—for six days she hadn't noticed the change of the month, but now it couldn't wait. Having run out of ways to put off answering, she realized that the phone might not ring forever and almost ran to the living-room side table.

"Hello?" Her voice was nervous, guarded. "Yes, it is."

After that it was mostly *"Ah's"* and *"I see's."* Even they can tell you a lot, of course. They told me—by their warily respectful tone—that it was Dr. Gaspard. Dr. Gaspard had called last night, while I was upstairs taking a long bath. When I'd come down, wrapped in one of Babushka's old dressing gowns, she had explained they were keeping Dad in the hospital overnight.

"Just for observation," she added.

"But I thought he wasn't hurt!" Had Ted Deakin been keeping the truth from me? "They said it was just a few bruises."

Babushka grimaced. She'd obviously decided to be straight with me, but it was an effort.

"I don't think it's the bruises they're interested in."

Not bruises? What, then?

I didn't need to ask that out loud. When a man starts rushing into fires and knocking people down for no reason, it's obvious what a doctor's going to think. And in Dad's case there were other things, too, from the time after Mum died. It was all there in the medical record: the mood swings, the prescriptions. But nothing like this before. Never like this.

I shifted my spoon around the milky shallows of a late breakfast and wished Babushka would hang up. On the radio some clergyman was talking about the power of love: "The power that can turn a rainy bus stop into paradise." A cozy parable. Happy Clappy singing. A different life was being lived in that plastic box, one that didn't touch mine at all. My world was bound by another kind of love, whose only power was to suffocate and spoil. Love was what I'd had enough of.

Jamie had eaten his heap of chocolate and left for the garden by the time Babushka made her good-bye noises. She put the receiver down and returned smiling, a conditional kind of smile. "They've decided your dad's well enough to come home."

I sat up straight. "Then they don't think he's—"

"No," she cut in. She didn't want to hear the word. "Apparently he was perfectly calm when Dr. Gaspard talked to him. He made a mistake, that's all. He honestly thought he saw someone trapped in the bonfire—they think it was a trick of the light. They discharged him an hour ago."

Did she really believe any of this? I wanted to ask her.

"But he still hit that man. Mel said he knocked him out."

"They're not going to take it any further. They didn't even call the police."

"Good." The expected word tolled flatly on my tongue.

"Yes, that's a relief!"

I took the bowl to the sink to rinse it out. I couldn't stand any more.

"Isn't it just! Now we can go on pretending!"

Babushka stared at me. "And what do you mean by that?"

It was a plea for silence. Babushka didn't really want an answer.

"Everything's back to normal! Dad's fine, I'm fine, we're all absolutely fine! No matter if his mind's being snuffed out like a candle. Let's just close our eyes and let it happen!"

"Petra!"

I threw the dishcloth at the nearest chair. "You'd rather lose your son than make a fuss? Someone's going to get killed!"

"I don't know what you're talking about!"

"That's fine, too!" I was already in the hall, struggling into my coat. "If I can't talk to you about it, maybe I can get through to him. Maybe it's not too late."

"Don't be ridiculous, Petra! Your father's had a traumatic night—it's rest he needs, not you bursting in like a wild thing."

Babushka had followed me into the hall, but there she stopped as if held by a force field. I glared at her. She wasn't being straight after all. She was trying on the voice of adulthood, pulling rank. But she knew. Deep down she knew. She wanted me to go and couldn't bring herself to say so: not with all that would have meant admitting. A bubble of contempt rose to my lips and burst.

"Go to hell!" I said.

The door to the workshop was ajar. For the last two days I had only seen it locked and out of bounds.

"Dad?"

I eased around the kitchen table, took a candle from the drawer, and lit it. The flame, still blossoming on the wick, flickered as I passed down the workshop steps into a pool of chilled air. Nothing moved. I didn't need to call again: Dad was not here. Why hadn't he come straight from the hospital? Again the flame shivered and shrank to a pinprick. I hadn't thought about it since the electricity went, but Dad's workshop (the garage, in a former life) had no windows at all. Even on the brightest day it would be like this—a crypt for unconsecrated Volvo parts. When he worked at those drawings, he'd have been doing it virtually in the dark.

I moved around the old chassis, steering a cautious path between spanners and jacks. As my eyes grew used to the gloom, a series of white rectangles became visible. Each was a sheet of draftsman's paper, pinned to the wall or laid across the floor. I knelt beside the nearest. It was a plan in Dad's careful manner of a large building. Exits and entrances were marked, everything reduced to squares and circles. Then I noticed its shape—long and two-armed, like a squashed letter *U*. I smiled to myself. Was this some future vision of Century Hall, hatched in Graham Cooke's brain? Or was it the Hall as it had been when Mr. Century knew it, in the years before the fire? The shadow of the future or of the past? Between them both, I thought, our present life had been squeezed to the merest sliver of a dream.

And Dad was fading from that dream.

The last sheet was still on the drawing board, in a corner hemmed in by crates and open drawers. Dad always felt safer behind the ramparts of this little fortress, but I gave myself a few bruises clambering toward it in the dark. I held the candle high above the paper. Around its border ran the Petroids, fat and cupid-faced. But now they had given up the building trade and discovered new vocations. Strange vocations—the kind Mr. Century had found inscribed in his ancestor's book, the kind Mel had laughed at. Petra striking a bell. Petra brandishing a sword. Petra shaking out incense, mouthing incantations. And there in the corner—Petra laid smiling in her grave.

I bit my lip. I could not look at this; couldn't stop either. I forced my gaze to the bottom of the paper, where a face lay lightly sketched out in a different style. Not a cartoon, but a portrait from life. Dad had never drawn me this way before, as a floating cloud of light and shadows. It was beautiful—beautiful. But it was not me. The face was small and pale like mine; like mine it was enveloped in dark folds of hair. But this was not my hair. It was black as night and shone with a gloss that ran its length like lightning. I stared at her, my black-haired sister, my sister-self—and knew it was the face of Eurydice Tremain.

I snatched the paper from the board and tore it into fragments. I was sick of it all. Sick of the slow, clammy pressure of someone else's mind upon my life, my home. I wanted to purge it and start again. I wanted to paint a red cross on the door. The little ball of anger I'd felt back at Babushka's seemed to swell inside me, and this time there was no way to choke it back. I knew where Dad had gone and that I had to find him there— and the knowledge was bitter in my mouth. I plunged up the steps into the kitchen. The room was tense with a strained silence, as if someone were trying hard to suppress a titter. At any moment a door or cupboard might fly open to reveal a dozen faces, twisted with laughter. But the cupboards stayed shut. I was quite alone.

It was only when I reached the traffic light at the bottom of The Rise that I stopped my bike and looked back. The rain clouds had passed, and all the houses shone once again with satin light. The road was streaked with rainbows where someone's engine had leaked oil. Everything was luminous. At the top of the road, where an old walnut tree used to be just visible above the garden sheds, there was now a triangular gap of sky. Never, I thought. I made myself a promise: I won't live there again. And as the lights turned green, I pushed the bike gently from the curb, in the direction of Century Hall.

The Hall had changed hands already. In only two days it had been roped and branded. The sign at the entrance to the court-yard was one I'd seen in other places around Cooper's Bridge.

A FRISCO DEVELOPMENT
IN ASSOCIATION WITH M. J. BALLARD
"MAKE FRISCO THE HEART OF YOUR HOME"
NO TRESPASSING

Heavy tires had driven ruts into the track from the Composers' Estate. Here in the courtyard, the trail ended at a yellow dump truck, with FRISCO written on the side in designer letters. There was no one about. A red plastic ribbon flapped across the entrance to the porch. I stepped over it and found the door locked.

The bell pull swung lazily beside my head, and I wondered whether to pull it. Would Dad even hear me if I did? I felt slightly sick as I thought of him, engrossed with visions of a dead woman. Part of me did not want to see him at all. But I knew I was going to try. Like a zombie I'd followed my hunch all the way back to Century Hall—pedaled across town, climbed the mossy track from Manor Lane. I'd come unthinkingly, with no better plan than the one I'd formed back at Babushka's, the plan that insisted I could talk Dad back into being himself despite everything. "Snap out of it, Dad! Pull yourself together!" With words like these, I hoped to exorcise the Darkling and appease sixty years of desire.

I looked back across the deserted courtyard. No one had seen me coming here. I was far, far from help.

I didn't ring the bell. There were other entrances, I knew; side doors, passages for tradesmen and servants. There were broken windows I could climb through. I would not leave. Even if Dad turned on me, I would face him. It would be useless, but I would do it anyway. And what might happen then I was too tired even to wonder.

I found my way in at the corner of the stable block. A set of wooden steps had been built up to a small platform beside the first floor. The door there was locked, but by setting my foot on the wooden rail of the platform, I could lean forward into the corner of the building and reach one of the windows at the front of the Hall. The latch was already broken. It swung open crookedly, and I kicked against the rail as I pulled myself inside headfirst. Behind me the wood splintered, and I felt my leg jar, then dangle free in midair. The edge of the sill scraped painfully along my ribs as I fell, half in and half out of the window. For a moment I was sliding back toward the cobbles. I grabbed hold of the sill, then hauled myself up and through the gap to land, winded, on the floor inside.

Slowly I got to my feet. I was in a large room, bizarre with nooks and alcoves. Floor and walls were bare, although there were trails in the dust where something heavy had recently been dragged. They led out into a corridor, and from there I saw doors to other rooms, all the way down to the ruby glow of a large stained-glass window. I walked toward it, opening each door in turn. Every room was empty. They were many sizes and shapes, but their bareness made them identical. As I walked, I kept looking over my shoulder, although I knew no one was following me. Perhaps I expected to see myself there: the ghost of Petra past, treading in the shadow at my heels.

To my right, the corridor turned into a much shorter passage. Here the only door was studded with bolts and metal florets. Gravity swung it open at my touch, to reveal a long, high room with a balcony. A metal rail ran parallel to some shelves, while a ladder led to the floor below. It was the library Mel and I had discovered, the one with the books and painted scrolls. But now I was standing on the balcony while beneath me a gray-suited man on his hands and knees pored over the patterns on the floor. He seemed to be searching for something he'd lost, but he was not Dad.

I stepped back, hitting the edge of the door with my heel. The sound juddered from end to end of the gilded room. The man jumped up in alarm and turned in my direction. As he stood, a tape measure snapped back into his hand. When he saw me, he was surprised—perhaps even frightened—but he speedily regained control of that obedient face of his and bent it into a smile of welcome.

"Good morning!" Graham Cooke exclaimed. "If it isn't my favorite dining partner. Spoiled any good suits lately?"

I didn't know what to reply.

"You shouldn't be here, you know," he continued. "Didn't you see the signs outside?"

I nodded.

"They're not there to make the place look pretty. It's a dangerous building, this. You should be careful. Woodworm, rats, dry rot—you name it. Accidents waiting to happen."

"I suppose you're right."

"Of course I'm right! We've got our work cut out, putting this lot to rights. You should trespass somewhere safer." He narrowed his gaze. I could see he was trying to guess why I'd come. Then he said in a conversational way, as he sidled over to the ladder, "I have to admit, though, this room's quite exceptional. It's going to be the atrium-*cum*-reception area, you know. We're after a combination of styles. Not just the usual moody Gothic, something a touch less baronial—Japanese, say. But you're looking lost."

"I'm looking for my father. Have you seen him?"

Graham climbed the ladder to the balcony as if this was the kind of question that could only be answered at eye level. "Am I your father's keeper?" he said. "I can only tell you where he *ought* to be, and that's at his desk. Do you mean to say he's not there?"

"You know he's not."

"How would I know that? I trust my colleagues." He frowned. "But perhaps my trust has been misplaced. Not at his desk? That's a serious dereliction of duty. A disciplinary offense, even."

I felt myself reddening. "Can't you drop it, just for once? This is serious!"

He stepped forward through the echo of my words. "I'm always serious when it comes to business." There was a new edge to his voice. "Now, suppose you tell me just what this is about?"

"It doesn't matter," I muttered, confused by his sudden closeness. "You couldn't help anyway."

"Touching confidence! Let's see how the clan McCoy has made out, shall we? Last night I get a strange call from Ted Deakin saying Dick's got into a fight and has been carted off to the hospital. This morning I arrive to discover someone's been mucking around on the site, and ten minutes later I find you wandering through a restricted area. Reliability isn't the word that springs to mind. What is it with your family? Do they put something in the water?"

"You're right, I must be mad! Otherwise I wouldn't even be talking to you."

"Oh, that's flattering. You're just trying to get on my good side."

"Can you blame me?"

He wiped the dust from his hands. "I don't know what I've done to make you hate me, anyway."

"What about Dad's job at Barlow's?"

"Haven't I *given* him a job?"

"After you lost him the last one!"

"Is that what he told you?" Graham pulled a hurt face, but this time I think he really was annoyed. "That's what you get for trying to help! The truth is, I stood up for him for a long time at Barlow's. They're not a charity, you know. He was paid to do a job of work, and he couldn't do it drunk or off his head— that's the bottom line. Face it, Petra! For a while there he couldn't have held down a job as a lollipop man. In case you hadn't noticed, your father was a wreck. You may think he's Leonardo da Vinci, but—well, just stop kidding yourself. I'm the best friend your dad's ever had. No one else would have taken him on."

"So you did it out of the kindness of your heart, right?"

"Right!"

Satisfied, he turned back toward the ladder.

"Don't forget. I know what you're really like."

The words came out so softly. I hardly knew I'd spoken. Graham rounded on me. "And what do you mean by that?"

"I don't need to spell it out."

"The hell you don't! If you've got something to say, say it."

"You remember." The words came hard. "That night—after Mum died."

"Now you're talking ancient history," he said, trying to sound bored. "I'll have to check my diary for this one."

"You were there. You came around to the house. I heard you downstairs."

"Did I? Perhaps I did. Your dad was in a state, and I consoled him over a glass or two. Or three or four. Oh, I led him astray all right—a man in his forties. If you want to blame me for that, go ahead."

"No, not for that."

I'd been lying in bed when the darkness parted like a curtain. A man stood there, framed in dusky light.

"Later—when you came upstairs. You pretended you were looking for the toilet. You'd got lost in the dark, you said."

"This is an interesting fairy tale. I suppose you get it from your Gran."

The shadow-man moved from the door toward me. I knew something was wrong, but I couldn't keep my eyes focused because of the drug. The drug they'd given me to calm me down.

"You sat down on the bed beside me. You said the cover had fallen off."

"You're crazy. I've never been in your room in my life."

I backed along the balcony but he followed me, step for step.

"Didn't I say you should be careful?"

A pretty thing. I'd soon get over it, he said, a pretty thing like me. He smoothed the blankets. A spume of whiskey words fouled the air.

One of the empty shelves tilted up at the pressure of my spine. Graham leaned forward, his lips level with my lips, and there was something new in his gaze. "But if I'd wanted to comfort you, too, where was the harm in that?"

He reached out to touch my shoulder. Instinctively I ducked

back along the balcony. Though he was right behind me, I managed to slam the door and fumble home the bolt. Along corridors and down stairways I fled, running as if he was just about to clamp his hand down on my neck. At last, short of breath, I stopped to rest. Graham could not have walked through a bolted door, I realized.

I was in a large room at the rear of the Hall. Like the rest, it was empty, except for a stack of paintings awaiting collection and a curtain half draped over them. A set of French windows curved in a bow, and then a terrace. I sank onto my heels and listened to the beating of my heart. Dad, Dad, where are you?

I went to the French window and tried the latch. It was stiff with disuse, but I managed to pull it free, the window sweeping back a bundle of leaves. As I stepped outside, I glanced up. The windows in the wall above dazzled me with the sun's reflection—I couldn't tell who might be watching. I grabbed at one of the urns that stood on the stone balustrade and hurriedly vaulted to the lawn below.

Too hurriedly—I hadn't seen the drop on the far side. As I fell my head cracked sharply against the flagstone path. At once a high-voltage pain shot through my brain, eyes, stomach. I rolled onto my knees, but the world rolled faster. The lawn with its sparse forest of fruit trees tilted drunkenly; then, as I raised myself, it finally settled. I loped along the path below the balustrade. I didn't care where I was going, so long as it was toward shelter. The air changed as I left the flagstones for grass. Dappled yellow light engulfed me, with leaves slushing underfoot. I was in the alley beside the burned wing of the Hall, where a thicket of sycamore had formed a narrow archway against the wall. Dizzy, I leaned against one of the window frames.

I was staring into the Temple of Pythagoras. Inside stood the remains of a wooden throne and behind that a stone pedestal. Scrubby weeds had pushed themselves up through the debris, adding to a scene of eerie drabness: stone, earth, and beams charred with black and gray.

And there was more. Someone was digging here—digging and weeping. A man was lurching from side to side as he strained to lift a large stone from the ground. He seemed so far away—beyond the gauze of pain, untouchable. It was Dad, and it was Mr. Century, and they were the same now, looking for the same miracle. Raising the dead. The resurrection men. He reached into a shallow trench and tenderly touched what he found inside. He was asking forgiveness. I could not see Eurydice Tremain, though surely she was there. She had died here once and then been made to live: a fading, sepia life.

I rested my head on my arms, tired by the explosions that fizzed against my eyes each time I tried to focus.

The sound of Graham's approach crept up on me like a dream. A distant cough. A door closing, too far away to be worth the effort of a thought. Then footsteps—closer, until the brute noise of them forced me into awareness. He was almost on top of me. He was walking down the flagstone path to the corner of the Hall. Too late, too late now. Nowhere to hide. I looked back at the temple: Dad was no longer visible. With a weary effort, I pulled myself through the blackened window frame and in, but couldn't suppress a hoarse gasp. The footsteps stopped. He had heard me, must have done. I limped half blind toward a pile of stones and flopped onto its far side. A moment later I was tumbling down a slope of dirt and broken wood into the trench Dad had revealed, where a brittle framework of bones was overhung with stone.

I must have lain there for years. Seasons circled overhead as I gazed up at that roofless patch of sky. Graham's footsteps came and went, and came again from the other side of the wing, where he could get in without the need for acrobatics. I followed them with a distant interest. They had nothing to do with me. I was hardly there at all. Then his face appeared above mine, swimming through the clouds. I didn't listen to the words he said, about short fuses, crossed lines—all human, humble things. Perhaps he was saying sorry. I grinned at him. I stroked out a twist of long black hair. And when he leaned down, his hand outstretched to pull me free ("Come on, come on, you're all right now"), and he saw Eurydice's white hand already clasped in mine, and his mouth went slack, I didn't mind.

He didn't hear my dad.

Suddenly Graham's head snapped back. Dad's right hand was pressed under his chin; the other held his throat. The fingers looked dirty and broken-nailed from all those excavations. But *he* was the one with dirty hands, Dad said.

"Take your filthy hands off her!"

Graham Cooke could not reply.

"You're not fit to touch a hair of her head!"

Did he mean Eurydice? I don't know. It doesn't matter any more. We are all invisible in the dark. Graham fought back, but Dad was stronger—he had the strength of two. When it was over, he wept. He squatted beside me with his head on his chest, and the sobs shook him back and forth. "I should have helped you before. I should have known . . . I should have thought . . . I've been so lonely, always . . . Find it in your heart . . . to forgive me?"

I did not listen to it all. The pain was a mist that muffled everything. I just turned my face aside, toward the other face beside me. How she had changed, Eurydice Tremain, since the day she had burst into a room full of lilies! How her pale beauty had waned! But her smile welcomed me as I met the coming darkness, and I knew I was safe at last.

15
The Way We Live Now

NOVEMBER 15, at eight-thirty in the morning, Eurydice Tremain's coffin was taken from the family plot in Tellerton churchyard. Jamie and Mig, who had ridden over specially, were watching from the churchyard wall. There were others, too, who gathered in the morning drizzle while the coroner's men did their work, though all they saw was the plastic screen the police had erected and a constable dripping peevishly in a cape. There was no skeleton inside, of course. Eurydice Tremain had been removed from her tomb some sixty years before and reburied in the Temple of Pythagoras. At this distance in time, said the coroner, it was unlikely that the full circumstances behind this bizarre act would ever be known.

The discovery added spice to a story that had already brought the national papers to Cooper's Bridge. Someone had played a sick joke. Someone was guilty of sacrilege. Was it the work of Satanists, the *Sun* wondered hopefully? I have the clippings in my bedroom, here in Babushka's attic. The arrest, the exhumation, the trial. It seems like another life now. Three years have yellowed the paper. I've cut my hair since that photo was taken. Everything's changed.

But I know that Mr. Century fooled the Tremains. I know he brought his beloved Eurydice back to the temple and made his peace with her in the end. I know because his story is my own. That long week joined us forever.

Dad knows it, too, I think—although he never says so in as many words. He is always cheerful when I see him. The last time was just a fortnight back. Lee was down from college, and we drove over in his Renault. It was late October, the kind of cloudless day you get sometimes, as if someone were wringing the last few drops of goodness from the year. Half an hour down the motorway toward the coast, then off into an unexpected valley of heath and open sky. When we arrived at the Sanctuary, I think Lee was surprised to find how pleasant it could be. Lawns neatly cut, hedges clipped, tennis courts. But he was still relieved when I said he should wait outside.

It's not easy to look at someone else's past.

Dad is already in the visitors' room. There's a smell of polish in here that makes me think of school on the first day of term, but I suppose they have to keep it clean. The chairs are the low-slung wooden kind, with plastic straps under the cushions. One of the straps on mine is missing, and I have a job not to fall through the middle. On the table between us sits a teapot and a plate of cookies.

"Shall I be mother?" Dad asks, and reaches for the pot. Recently he's acquired a domesticated way of speaking, which I find hard to take. It's the culture of the place, Dr. Gaspard says. He pours the tea and starts telling me about his latest butterfly sighting—an Adonis Blue, quite rare. He is full of gossip and talks of people I have never met as if they are old friends: Bernard, Lemmy, Brother Andrew who buys him special ink for his technical pens, the splendid Eileen with her preference for Ajax over Flash.

Eventually I show him the paper I've brought, the latest *Argus*. It's a bit of an experiment, this, and I'm not sure how he's going to take it.

"I thought you might be interested," I say, folding it casually to the right page. He takes the paper out of politeness and briefly scans it, then smiles at me, puzzled.

"See, Century Hall Hotel is opening at last," I explain, and point out the feature ad. It takes up half the page. At the top is a frontal view of the Hall, complete with the fully restored Tremain Wing. Two or three people of unknown age and sex wander about the romantic courtyard cobbles, while another parks a car in what used to be the stable block. "Century Hall Hotel offers unrivaled luxury for the executive and business traveler," I read aloud. "Set in thirty acres of—blah, blah, blah, you don't want to know about that. Ah!" (This is it, keep your voice steady.) "At the end of a long day, why not relax with a cocktail or one of our fine selection of wines in the Graham Cooke Bar?"

Dad stiffens. "Graham Cooke Bar?"

"Ballard named it in his honor," I explain.

Well, Petra, now you've said it. Sink or swim. His fingers travel slowly toward his knees. There they interlock and hug tight while he leans forward over the table. His expression is troubled, but strangely unfocused, too. Slowly it gives way to a wide smile. "That Graham Cooke! He'll be demanding free drinks there for life, knowing him!"

No. Never let him get away with this—so says Dr. Gaspard.

"He's dead, Dad. Remember?"

The smile fades. "Oh yes, I'd forgotten." He looks sad briefly, then gives a wry shake of the head and is smiling once again. "Trust me to forget a thing like that! I'll be forgetting my own head next!"

He asks after Babushka. "She never visits," he complains.

"That's not quite true."

"She hasn't been to see me since—well, I can tell you exactly . . ." He takes a diary from his back pocket, licks his finger, and flicks through it efficiently. It is last year's diary though, and its pages are blank. "Boxing Day, I think it was," he cries, spotting the words printed on the page in front of him. "How do you like that?"

"She's very busy, Dad. She has a lot to do, with me and Jamie. It's not been easy for her."

Babushka gives me funny looks sometimes. Does she hate me, despite all she says and does? What is she thinking of?

"She's got a new book coming out, did you know? Not a romance this time. The heroine's a detective called Messalina Morningcloud. She lives in a gypsy caravan and goes up and down England, solving murders."

"At her age? I'd have thought she'd be taking it easy."

"Not Babushka, Dad! Messalina Morningcloud—she's the youngest daughter of the Duke of Marshalsea."

We have a good laugh about this. The door behind Dad opens, and a mild-looking man in a clerical collar pokes his head in and gives me the ten-minute signal.

"I don't know why she moved away from Tellerton," Dad

sighs. "We had such good times when I was a kid."

"It was a long way from mine and Jamie's schools," I point out. That was considered important at the time. We needed some continuity for the good of our health. The new house in Vermeer Drive suits us very well; besides, I love my little attic room. "I was in the middle of my exams, remember?"

"Oh yes, I was so proud when I heard about your results! Did I remember to congratulate you?"

"Of course you did, Dad. You sent me that lovely bunch of lilies. That wonderful scent!" Beautiful they were, straight from the hospital garden. I hope he got permission. "They were more than I deserved."

"Nothing's more than you deserve, my dear." He looks at me with simpering affection.

"Oh don't, Dad!"

"I know what I know," he declares, folding his arms. "I know how hard you worked." He leans forward and adds fervently: *"You are my morning star."*

"Mel did even better," I say, sidestepping this observation. "Dr. Gaspard's talking about Cambridge. Though Mel would rather slit her wrists, she says. You know how it is: he wants her to do medicine; she fancies her chances as a starving poet."

"That one's so sharp she'll cut herself," he nods. "You're worth ten of her."

"I'm not, Dad. I'm really not."

But his face has that sudden glassy look, and I know he's no longer here. "Ten at least," he repeats, but the words don't mean anything this time. He's tripped a wire somewhere in his head and sent a shutter crashing down.

There's no point in staying, so I take his hand and squeeze it briefly. "Bye, Dad. I'll visit again soon."

"I'd like that very much," he says.

I call the Brother who showed me in and make my way across the black-and-white-tiled lobby to the steps where Lee is waiting, crouched in a frayed jean jacket. Lee leaps up when he sees me and looks instinctively at his watch. "You were quick. I thought you'd be a while yet."

"I didn't want you to get bored." I fish my velvet cap from my pocket and arrange it in the reflection of the brass plate on the door. Lee nuzzles up against me, but I'm not in the mood.

He gets the message. "I guess it's kind of hard," he suggests. "To see him like that, I mean."

"Kind of." Because it kind of is. "Imagine it—just small talk and cookies, forever and ever, amen. No brilliant career for him!"

"What's that supposed to mean?" Lee seems to think this nonsense is directed against him, somehow.

"Nothing. Nothing at all." I kiss him in apology. "This place jangles my nerves, that's all. Come on, let's take a drive."

"Where do you want to go?"

"Hengistbury Head." The smell of polish has got into my clothes. "Some fresh air will do us good."

We walk past the fountain to the car park, where the Renault is sitting in the shade of a huge cedar. It needs a wash, as usual. Lee's new bumper sticker is already nearly illegible. CYBERPUNKS DO IT IN THEIR HEADS. There are dozens of stickers plastered over the body and the windows. Anyone waiting behind Lee in a traffic jam knows all his opinions well before the lights change. The strange thing is, he *wants* them to know! He lives a life without secrets! Which to me is inexplicable. Perhaps that's why I love him.

"It won't *be* forever, anyway." One hand searches for the keys, the other for me across the top of the car. "You told me yourself what the doctor said."

"I know, I know. I'm not complaining, Lee. He's never been so happy."

That sounds a strange thing to say, but it's true, you know. He never has.

Once we're in the car, I put in a tape and turn the volume up. *The Welfare Cheats Live.* We drive down half a mile of landscaped lawn to the gate, where a man in a peaked cap nods and smiles and presses a button inside his weatherproof box. The electric barrier rises with the slow deliberation of an ax, then, somewhere behind us, returns to execute the empty air. I think I hear the Sanctuary bell. But by that time we are far away and moving down the open valley to the sea.